THE
NURSE'S
LIE

BOOKS BY DANIEL HURST

As I turn a corner, I'm suddenly confronted with another nurse. She looks me right in the eyes, causing every cell in my body to tell me that this is it. This is where it's over. This is where I get punished for being here and pretending to be a proper nurse.

But nothing happens. The other nurse just smiles at me before walking past, as if she didn't see a ghost. Okay, so I'm not dead, so I'm not really a ghost, but I feel like one, haunting this hospital, destined for doom, because the longer I'm here, the less time I have to back out of this. Except I'm not backing out, and I know I'm close to where I need to be now – I see a police officer chatting to a doctor in the distance.

That police officer is here to see the same patient.

But I need to make sure I see them first.

I walk past the police officer and the doctor, either one of whom could suddenly ask me a question and cause me to have a panic attack. A simple question like, 'Where are you going?' would be enough to do it. Then, when they saw me crumble, they'd know I was a fraud, and the doctor would sound the alarm while the officer would reach for one of two things.

His handcuffs.

Or his gun.

I can't believe I'm doing this. I can't believe I thought this was best. I can't believe I could be responsible for giving nurses all over the world such a bad name. They don't deserve it.

This uniform, and this job, should be respected.

But I'm about to make it feared.

It didn't have to be like this. Things could have been so different. As it is, I'm going to do the one thing that a person wearing this uniform should never do. Hell, I'm going to do the one thing no person should ever do, regardless of their profession.

I am going to take a life.

Even worse, I'm not going to regret it for one second.

BEFORE

ONE

DARCY

I check the address scribbled on the napkin in my hand before looking up and confirming that I'm in the right place. I think this is where I'm supposed to be: 31 Oceanview Parade, and it is actually a fairly accurate representation of the surrounding area. Some streets have fancy names that fail to live up to the glamour of them upon arrival, but this one is as advertised. There's a view of the ocean from this property, and I savour a few seconds of staring at the serene sea behind me before I stuff the napkin in my pocket and head for the door.

The napkin originated from the café where I was working a trial shift. I was given this address by a handsome male customer who clearly took pity on me and my poor coffee-making skills. I'd been dropping things all morning, and earning unwanted glares from my manager, so maybe the customer had detected that I was in trouble. Either that or he could tell that I was desperate for another job, something I'd be better at, something more meaningful than serving hot drinks to frustrated Floridians. The sympathetic customer chatted with me and was friendly at a time when I really needed it, so by the time he said he wanted something from me, I was inclined to provide it.

Whatever the case, he gave me this address and told me he needed my help, help that would be better paid than the 'help' I was providing at the coffee shop and, as I'm here now, I guess I'm willing to offer it.

This place is one of many condominiums in this state – plush high-rise apartment buildings mostly home to retirees who flock to Florida for the warmer weather and cheaper prices, aiming to enjoy their remaining years in pleasant surroundings. It's certainly pleasant here, and while it might be cheaper than other places around the country, it must still be pricey if the building itself is anything to go by. I look up at the tall building and see balconies that must offer even better views of the ocean, as well as several sports cars parked nearby and plentiful palm trees in the surrounding gardens. I'd be more than happy to retire here myself, if not for the fact that I'm not even forty yet. Even if I was older, I hardly have the kind of money that would afford me a luxurious type of retirement.

As I reach the door, I'm still undecided as to whether or not this is a good idea. I don't know if I should be here or if I'm even capable of doing what I'm supposed to do when I go inside, but it's either this or I go back to that café and beg for another chance. At least here I'll earn good money – all cash in hand, in fact, which is perfect – and it's also likely that I'll have a much better boss.

The good-looking guy who wrote down this address is called Parker, and I'm here to meet him and his father, Joe. Parker has asked for my help, though he's not the one who needs it. It's his dear dad that requires assistance, and I'm about to find out just how much support he needs once this door is opened.

Taking a deep breath, I press the buzzer and wait for some-body to let me in. I assume it will be Parker, and I hope it will be, so he can talk me through exactly what the job involves. I'm also a little excited to see him again, though any crush I might be developing on him should probably be cooled if I want to keep this arrangement professional.

'Hello?'

It's Parker's deep voice that I hear clearly through the intercom, and I smile before answering.

'Hey, it's Darcy,' I say in my most cheerful tone.

'Great! Come in,' Parker replies enthusiastically before I hear the lock release and the door opens.

I step inside the reception area and, despite treading lightly, my footsteps still echo loudly off the marble floor in this cavernous reception area. I wonder how many people live here in these units and, as I reach the elevators, I see a few of them coming out. Two couples, all in their seventies, and all sporting sun-kissed skin. The men are wearing flowery shirts that wouldn't look out of place in Hawaii, while their partners are wearing designer sunglasses and have the straps of expensive handbags slung over the shoulders of their summer dresses. Whatever these people did for work in their younger years, they certainly seem to know how to enjoy their retirement, and as I watch them leave the building, presumably destined for the beach, I wish I had one ounce of their apparent ease and contentment. As it is, I'm a ball of nerves, and not just because this is my first day in a new job. It's my natural state, always anxious, and nothing seems to make it better. Not the sunny climate in this part of the world, not the prospect of a well-paying job, and not even my young age in comparison to the elder residents around here. I don't quite know why I feel like this every day when I wake up, but such is my paranoia I almost feel like I'm better off not knowing.

Parker told me, by way of writing it on my napkin, that his father lives on the fifth floor, so I push the button with the big five on it, and the elevator starts ascending. At least I think it's going up, but it's such a smooth ride that it's hard to tell. Seconds later the doors slide silently open, and I see that I have risen up above street level to reach a corridor with several doors, and a large glass window at the end offering an even better view of the sea than I had a few minutes ago.

After consulting the address on my napkin again, I find the door with the number thirty-one on it and take a deep breath before raising my hand to knock. Before I can, the door flies open, and I see a devilish grin staring back at me. It's Parker, and he's clearly pleased to see me, which only makes the butterflies in my stomach flutter even faster.

'You found us!' he says, still grinning, and the only time my eyes move away from his are when I momentarily glance at the tanned biceps poking out of his blue T-shirt. As if I've been lucky enough to find a well-paying job for a guy who looks like this.

'Yeah, it was no trouble to find,' I reply, secretly hoping that he's as pleased to see me as I am to see him, but I think he is. Or maybe he's glad that he now has the extra help he so desperately needs. As he invites me in, I remind myself that I'm here because he told me he was struggling to manage things on his own. Then I see the reason for that struggle.

Parker's father is sitting in an armchair in front of the television, his back to us, though I doubt it's because he's being rude. He's probably too tired to turn around, or too occupied with the baseball game on screen, or maybe he's even asleep and doesn't know I'm here at all yet. But I guess I'll be meeting him officially any moment now, and I'm eager to make a good first impression when I do. That's because if this is going to work, he needs to like me. Otherwise, I doubt I'll be invited back here again, which means I can kiss goodbye to the money I desperately need to earn, as well as kiss goodbye to getting to know Parker any better.

'I'll make you a drink in a moment, but first, would you like to meet my father?' Parker asks me quietly, and I nod nervously, which I guess he picks up on based on what he says next.

'Don't worry. He knows you're coming, and he knows to be on his best behaviour,' Parker tells me before approaching the armchair, and I slowly follow.

'Dad? Darcy is here. Remember I told you she was coming round. Say hello.'

The seventy-three-year-old man in the armchair, with the bald head and freckled cheeks, reluctantly takes his attention off the sport on TV and turns to look at me. When he sees me, I smile at him.

'Hi Joe, I'm Darcy. It's a pleasure to meet you,' I say, extending my hand and expecting him to take it. But he doesn't. He looks me up and down before shaking his head.

'Who are you?'

Parker goes to speak, but I let him know that I've got this, kneeling down beside the armchair so I'm more on the patient's level.

'I'm your new nurse,' I say gently. 'I'm here to help you.'

'You don't look like a nurse,' Joe replies gruffly. 'Where's your uniform?'

Joe's got a good point. I'm not wearing a uniform, and that's because I don't currently own one. I could make up an excuse, or justify my position here, or simply say anything to let him know that I'm the right person to look after him while his son is at work. But I don't, because I don't want to start off things by lying to this man and, right now, I'm not even sure I could look after myself.

The truth is, I'm afraid that Joe might be right. I don't look like a nurse. I don't even feel like one. Yet, I'm here, trying to be one.

But should I be?

Or am I making a big mistake?

TWO

I'm going to need to overcome my awkward start with Joe and put his concerns at ease, as well as any concerns that Parker might have had about hiring me in the first place. I'm aiming to do that by sitting with Joe while he watches the baseball game, so I can chat to him about the action on screen, as well as ask him a few things about his personal life. I'm not just going to enquire about him as a person to be nice; it's vital that I get to know him better, as the more I know and understand him, the better care I can give him when his son isn't around.

Parker has mostly left the pair of us to it since our initial introduction, making himself busy elsewhere in the spacious apartment, so I've got the freedom to engage with Joe, which is important if I am to bond with him. I'm hoping to get plenty of interaction with Parker too during my time here, but at the moment, his father is the more pressing priority. All Parker told me before I got here was that his dad was in the early stages of dementia and needed somebody to keep an eye on him, before he inevitably requires full-time care and is forced to leave his home and move into a facility with other patients just like him. I can see why both father and son are desperate to delay that fairly grim inevitability for as long as possible, because this is a lovely home that Joe has here.

The apartment is very modern, no doubt built recently and, as such, it's equipped with plenty of mod-cons to make life easier for those who reside here. A strong air-conditioning unit keeps the place cool, while the blinds over the windows are electronically operated, perfect for when the sun is glaring through and those inside need some respite from the brightness. There is a large fridge in the kitchen, a spacious shower with handrails in the bathroom and the TV is big enough to keep Joe's attention even when the game pauses for a commercial break. Best of all, there is the balcony, offering a stunning view of the beach below, with all the tourists sunning themselves on the sand, and the sea beyond that, where I can spot Jet Skis bouncing across the water, driven by laughing thrill seekers wearing life vests. Wherever Joe ends up after this, he's unlikely to have access to all these amenities, or a view as good as this one, so I guess it's up to me to help him as much as possible, to hopefully delay the need for him to leave here. His place is much nicer than mine, a run-down apartment with noisy neighbours, but that's my problem. His problem is hanging onto this lovely place that he's got.

'That was a good catch,' I say to Joe after we've watched the outfielder on TV claim the baseball in his glove, but Joe says nothing, meaning I've still got plenty of work to do to win him over.

'It's a lovely place you have,' I say, looking around again. 'How long have you lived here?'

'You don't have to pretend to be interested,' Joe replies glumly.

'But I am interested,' I reply.

'Interested in me, or interested in getting paid?'

'I'm here to help you.'

'You're here because it's your job.'

This might not be the best line of conversation to continue along, so I switch lanes.

'Okay, I'll tell you about my place then,' I say. 'I live in an apartment too, but it's much smaller than this one. It's nowhere near as nice. I don't have a view like yours, but I wish I did. I'm very jealous.'

Joe scoffs at that, which is not what I was hoping to hear.

'What's wrong?' I ask him.

'You're not jealous of me,' he says quietly. 'How could you be? You're young. You're healthy. I'm neither of those things.'

Joe probably thinks he has me beat there, but while I can't argue with the first point, because I am much younger than he is, I wouldn't say I'm healthy, not with the way I struggle to remember things too. But, as well as that, there is one other area where he trumps my current situation.

'You're right about me being younger than you, but you have something I don't.'

'What's that?' Joe mumbles. I must be making progress, because he turns to look at me rather than the baseball for the first time since I sat down.

'You are close to your family,' I reply. 'Your son is here, and you get to see him whenever you want to. I don't get to see my family whenever I want to.'

'Why not?'

While I might be making progress with Joe by talking along these lines, I'm regretting it now – this is something I shouldn't really be talking about.

'It's complicated,' I say meekly.

'Try me.'

Joe is very intrigued, probably because he gets the impression my personal life is more interesting than his own, or at least more interesting than the baseball game. But I've already said too much, so I try to change the subject.

'Parker said you still enjoy going for walks, so I was thinking we could make a habit of it. Maybe I'll treat you to ice cream at the beach one day, if you like?'

I expect Joe to like that idea, or simply to go back to watching the game, but he doesn't allow me to drop it that easily.

'What's the issue with your family? Why won't you tell me?'

'It's nothing,' I try, but it's well past the point of me hiding it, and Joe still has the mental faculties to know it.

'You've got a secret, haven't you?' he asks confidently, but I'm not sure if it's a question or a statement.

'Excuse me?'

'You can't fool me. I might be losing my marbles, but there's still a few cogs in here that are working,' he says, tapping the side of his head. 'I'm intrigued to find out what your secret is, so I guess you can stay. But don't think you're the only one with something to hide.'

Joe turns back to the game now, but I'm confused.

'What do you mean the only one?'

'Other people have secrets too,' Joe responds casually.

'You mean yourself?' I ask, but Joe shakes his head.

'No, not me. Somebody else in this apartment. Somebody you think is being nice to you, but I'm telling you to be careful, and you'd do well to heed my warning.'

'You mean Parker?' I ask, though it should be obvious, because he's the only other one here with us. I look around for him but I can't see him, so he must be in the bedroom or bathroom. But I'm confused. As far as I can tell, Parker seems like a very honest and genuine guy.

'Do you know why you're here?' Joe asks me, which seems like a strange question. 'I mean, really here.'

'To help you,' I reply, but Joe scoffs.

'There's no helping me, not anymore. No, you're here because it's helping my son.'

'I guess it gives him a break,' I suggest, but Joe laughs again.

'My boy does not need a break,' he says, suddenly becoming stern again. 'He leaves me here by myself most of the time. It's been that way since my wife died.'

I was wondering if and how I would broach the awkward subject of his late wife. Parker briefly mentioned this when we met, but Joe has gone ahead and done it for me, although he's done so in a way that makes Parker look bad.

'I'm sure your son doesn't leave you here all day,' I say. 'He's just busy. He has a job.'

'Oh, he's busy all right. But he's doing a lot more than working.'

'What do you mean?'

'Never mind. Drop it,' Joe says, and he holds up his hand to make it clear that he's done talking about this. But I'm not, so should I push it further?

'Do you want to talk about your wife?' I offer, trying to come at it from a different angle, but Joe shakes his head.

'No.'

'Why not?'

'Because the precious and personal memories I can recall are for me and me alone. Not to be shared with you, whoever the hell you are.'

This is not going well at all, and I'm wondering if I'm going to bother coming back here or if Joe or Parker will even want me to return. Maybe Parker misread me when we met and he presumed I'd be good at this. Maybe whatever caring, nurturing side he saw in me was false, and I'm not the right person for this job, even though I desperately need the money and I have no other options at present. Maybe I'd also be better off leaving it because, from the sounds of it, Parker might not be the most trustworthy guy either. But who do I trust more? The kind stranger who gave me this job, or the unfortunate patient who has memory issues? I feel bad but I opt to trust the younger man, though it might not just be a practical decision. I don't just need money; I also need a friend. I need company. I need more from life than what I'm currently getting, and maybe Parker is the solution to all of that. He has been nothing but good to me, so it would be disrespectful of me to not trust him.

I might be thinking with my heart rather than my head, but whatever it is, I'm staying.

For now, at least.

If only to find out if Parker has a secret worth hiding.

THREE

'How are we getting along?' Parker asks us both as he re-enters the room five minutes later, looking relaxed and not at all like a man with a secret, like his father alluded to earlier.

'Yeah, okay, I think,' I say, but I guess it's Joe's opinion that matters to his son the most, so I await the verdict nervously.

'She's fine,' Joe says with a shrug, thankfully, though a little condescendingly too.

'That's a relief,' Parker says, that relief evident all over his face. I'm pleased he's happy, although I'm still a little unsettled about what his father just said about him. But there's no time to ponder that any more as Parker speaks again.

'I've got to go out and run a few errands now, so am I okay to leave you guys to it?'

'Erm, sure,' I say before looking at Joe to check if it's okay with him.

'See you later, son,' he says quietly, his eyes still on the TV, and Parker gives me a nod of thanks and heads for the door. I almost call out to him, to get him to wait a moment, because I feel like there are a few things we need to discuss, but he's quickly gone and now it's just me and Joe. I wasn't expecting the pair of us to be left alone so soon after my arrival, and it feels a little abrupt, but maybe it's a good thing.

'What were you talking about before?' I ask Joe, probing, once Parker has definitely gone. I'm intrigued, even if it is most likely over something silly and innocent. 'You were suggesting your son has a secret.'

'Forget about it,' Joe says. He makes a sad joke. 'Oh no, wait, I'm the one who forgets things around here.'

He chuckles to himself, but the truth behind what he said means, I assume, that his humour is merely a coping mechanism for his declining mental functions. But was he making an attempt at a joke, or was he actually hinting that he knows more about me than I realise? After all, I know he's not the only one who has memory issues here, though I would not openly admit that to him or his son if I can help it. I have my troubles too, but best to keep them to myself.

There's no way Parker or Joe can know about me or my past. I can't even remember most of it, which actually helps, and nobody else around here knows it either. That's why I'm here. Because I'm a total stranger in these parts.

It's safer for me that way.

While I'm definitely not the biggest sports fan in the world, I sit patiently with Joe until the baseball game finishes, which seems to take forever. There's also a reminder of Joe's problems when, at one point during the eighth inning of the game, he picks up his phone and tries to turn up the volume on the television, rather than using the remote control sitting on the table in front of him. I awkwardly hand him what he needs, and he stares at me for a moment before using it, but I say nothing about it because I don't want to reinforce his mistake or make him feel bad.

'How about a sandwich?' I suggest when the game is over. 'I'll make it.'

'I'm not a complete invalid,' Joe replies sternly, which makes me feel foolish, so then we go to make a sandwich together. But I feel like I'm walking on metaphorical eggshells while we're in the kitchen, and I'm trying to gauge exactly how much help this man needs. Should I use the sharp knife instead of him in case he cuts himself, or is that silly of me to worry about such a thing? What about him carrying a glass? Will he drop it and cut his feet?

I realise that I need to take a deep breath and relax. It's going to feel weird for a while yet, me being here, but I remind myself of my job title – I'm a home nurse now – whenever I start to feel uncomfortable. Parker says I am here for his peace of mind as much as to help his father, so the more I can do around here, the better.

As Joe and I work together to make a salami sandwich, I think about how I met Parker. It was a fateful meeting. I was toiling away behind the counter of a beachfront café, struggling through my second trial shift, serving hot drinks to thirsty tourists and locals, when I accidentally gave Parker, the customer, the wrong order. He'd ordered a latte, but I gave him a macchiato, and while he was polite when he called me out on my mistake, I became increasingly flustered and ended up spilling the next drink I made all over the floor.

Drawing the ire of the manager who had given me the opportunity at a full-time job, and aware that I was out of my comfort zone, I had given up and quit before I was fired. It seemed a foolish, impulsive thing to do at the time, because I needed the money, as well as the safety net of being employed, but I couldn't do it. I fled the café and went to the beach where I sat with my head in my hands and tried to figure out where my life was going. It was a thankless task with no potential resolution in sight, so it was surely a good thing that my thoughts were interrupted by the man taking a seat on the sand beside me.

I'd looked up to see Parker, holding his correct drink this

time, but he was holding another coffee too and, politely, he offered the spare one to me.

'Tough day?' he asked after I gratefully accepted the free drink.

I nodded.

'I think you were destined for somewhere better than that place anyway,' he had said then, which made me laugh, because I wasn't sure I agreed, but it was nice to hear it all the same. 'So, what is it you really want to do?'

'I don't know,' is all I had been able to reply to that, but Parker hadn't been prepared to leave it there.

'I don't usually make a habit of taking pity on the people who serve me the wrong coffee, but I can make an exception for you,' he had said. 'But I might be able to help you. Or rather, maybe you can help me.'

'What do you mean?'

'I've got a bit of a problem. It's my father. He's in his seventies now, and sadly he's got dementia.'

'I'm so sorry,' I'd offered, but Parker just shrugged to show that he had already come to terms with the diagnosis.

'I'm trying to save up the money to send him to somewhere where he can get the care he needs, preferably before he gets much worse,' he'd gone on. 'But it's not easy. Nursing homes are so expensive, so it could be a while until I get the money together.'

'Is your mom still around?' I had asked then, but Parker had shaken his head.

'No, she died last year.'

'I'm sorry,' I'd said again, and it seemed like I'd found somebody having a worse time of things than me.

'Here's how I see it,' Parker had said after a sip of his coffee. 'You need a new job and I need somebody to help me look after my dad. So how about it? Do you want to help me? I'll pay you, of course. I can do cash too, if that's better.'

Money sounded great, but did the job?

'How do you mean help? Like a carer?'

'You could call it that. Or nursing. It would be informal, of course, but it's still the same kind of thing.'

'Nursing?'

'Sure, why not? I can see you have a caring side, and that's all you need. Who knows, maybe you should have been a nurse in another life, and this is your true calling.'

I'd pondered that when he said it and it was weird, but something about it seemed to touch a nerve. Parker must have noticed, because he doubled down on his offer, and when he told me I could start as soon as I wanted to, I had found it difficult to say no. Or maybe it was the way he looked sitting beside me on the beach, tanned, toned and handsome, showing me attention, helping me when I had nobody else in the world looking out for me.

So I said yes and that's how I ended up here.

'You're thinking about him, aren't you?' Joe suddenly says, snapping me out of my daydream.

'Sorry?' I say, refocusing on finishing the sandwich I'm supposed to be making.

'Don't waste your time. He's taken.'

Joe picks up the plate with his sandwich and carries it back to his armchair, so I quickly finish making mine and follow him.

'What are you talking about?' I ask as I retake my seat.

'My boy. He's got a girlfriend, so don't entertain any ideas of you and him because it won't happen. Nor should it.'

'I wasn't—'

'My brain might be broken, but there's nothing wrong with my eyes,' Joe says with a shake of the head. 'You look like a lovesick puppy when he's around you, but I'm saying you need to snap out of it.'

I'm shocked that Joe has been able to read me so easily, and then I fear that his son might have done the same. But if Parker has noticed that I like him then he hasn't said anything. He's certainly not as blunt as his father, and it's hard to tell if Joe's bluntness is a trait of his personality or a symptom of his condition. But it's not just the fact I've been called out that has shaken me a little; it's the fact that Joe has told me his son is already in a relationship. I didn't know that, not that it's any of my business. But has Parker deliberately been keeping that fact about his personal life quiet, or has it just not come up yet in conversation? Or is he withholding it because it doesn't suit him to reveal it? Maybe he knew he'd have a better chance of convincing me to do this job for him if I thought he was a handsome, single stranger rather than a taken man. If he does have a girlfriend, I guess that means he is out of bounds for me in terms of anything beyond friendship developing, because I wouldn't wish to steal him away from anybody. I shouldn't even be bothered he's taken, and it's bugging me that I am.

I'm overthinking things again, but sadly, I'm not the only one whose brain is struggling. Not too long after Joe has finished his sandwich, he gets up to go to the kitchen, and when I ask him what he's looking for, he says it's time for lunch and he needs a sandwich. He's obviously forgotten he's eaten, and while it could be worse and he could be forgetting to eat altogether, it's just another sign that his mental faculties are on the wane. With that in mind, I try to forget about Parker and what his father has told me about him since I got here and focus on being the best help I can for Joe. I make him another sandwich, one he barely touches in the end because he's obviously full from the first one, and then I try to run through a few memory exercises with him, though he quickly gets bored of that and ends up falling asleep in his chair.

I sit with him for the rest of the day, most of which he spends snoozing. At least I'm here, watching out for him and doing what his son asked me to do. Pretty soon, Parker will be home, and I can't wait, though it's not because I want to finish here and go home myself. Why would I wish to be back in my tiny apartment, alone again?

It's because I have a few questions to ask the man who gave me this job.

The answers to those questions will resolve whether or not I can trust him. And whether or not I'll come back here again.

FOUR

It's not the most professional thing I could have done at work, but while Joe was sleeping, I actually fell asleep for a short while myself. Maybe it was the heat from the sun coming through the window in front of the balcony, or maybe it was the opposite and the coolness of the air conditioning made it the perfect temperature to induce sleep. Whatever it was, my eyes closed while Joe's were closed and the pair of us slept, although when I wake up, I hope the man in the armchair beside me achieved a better state of rest than I did. That's because I had another one of my nightmares, the ones that always seem to plague me, and the ones I blame the most for my current levels of tiredness and paranoia.

This particular bad dream was similar to my other ones in that I was wearing a nurse's uniform. There's always a medical theme to my nightmares, not to mention the random flashbacks I sometimes get too, but I'm not sure why that is. All I am sure about is that, when they're over, I feel very, very unsettled. Perhaps it's the sense I get that the uniform does not belong on me, or it could be the feeling that something terrible is going to happen the longer I stay with a patient or be around others in the medical profession. Or it could be much simpler than that. It could just be the vision my nightmares always end with. The vision of the dead woman, the one who lies on a bed beside me and stares at me with vacant eyes, one arm outstretched and hanging over the edge of the bed towards me, as if she needs me to help her, but it's already too late.

I couldn't help her.

Or I chose not to.

Or I possibly even killed her myself.

I rub my eyes and do the best job I can of making it look like I wasn't asleep, so that Joe won't notice when he wakes up and report back to his son about it. But thankfully, Joe is still asleep when I wake, so I haven't been caught napping on the job. I check the time and see that it's almost five and I wonder when Parker will be back. As if by magic, I hear a key turning in the lock a moment later and the door to the apartment opens.

Have I been locked in here this whole time? I wonder. I assumed the door was open, but I guess not. I suppose I can add that to the list of things I need to chat to my new employer about.

I get up off the sofa and leave the sleeping Joe while I go to see his son, and when I find Parker walking in carrying a bag of groceries, I put my finger to my lips.

'He's asleep,' I whisper to let Parker know to keep the noise down so as not to wake his dad, but Parker doesn't seem too bothered about that.

'Oh, I should have told you. He sleeps quite a lot. Easy job, huh?'

Parker smiles at me before placing the grocery bag down on the kitchen counter, and then he starts unpacking it, pulling out cartons of fruit juice and a box of cereal, still not making much effort to keep the noise down.

'How's today been?' he asks me as he finishes unpacking.

'It's been okay, I think,' I reply as I glance back towards Joe. I can just about see the top of his head in the chair, and he isn't moving yet, so I guess he's not been disturbed – this is my chance to talk to Parker in private.

'But I'm not sure I'm the right person for this job,' I add, and Parker stops moving around.

'Sorry?'

'I'm not sure this is going to work, so maybe it's best if you find somebody else.'

'But I don't want anybody else. You're perfect for this, I just know it.'

Parker approaches me, looking me in the eyes and smiling and, there it is again, that feeling inside that tells me I'm drawn to this man and the idea that something might happen between us one day. But I remember what Joe said: Parker has a girl-friend, so however he's trying to make me feel right now, I know it's not genuine. He doesn't like me in the same way I like him, and maybe he's manipulating me into doing this job for him so he can have an easier life with his partner.

Am I being used? I'm being paid, but still, that doesn't mean I can't be used at the same time.

'What did my dad say?' Parker asks me, rolling his eyes.

'Sorry?'

'He must have said something to make you have second thoughts. So what was it?'

I know it won't be very cool of me to mention the girlfriend, so I forget about that part, but there is the part about Joe telling me that his son has a secret. Should I broach that subject?

'Nothing,' I reply weakly, as that's far easier than saying something uncomfortable.

'Are you sure? I know what Dad's like. He's always spoken his mind before, but it's not such a good thing now that his mind isn't what it was, if you know what I mean. He's said some crazy things to me over the last few months. He even accused me of killing Mom once, which is ridiculous, but the doctors warned me that patients like him can come out with all sorts of upsetting things as they get more and more confused.'

Of course that's it. Joe's condition is causing him to say strange things, things that probably aren't true, and I really need to remember that. He could be exaggerating about Parker having a secret, or just plain lying, and he might even be lying about Parker having a girlfriend too.

'Here,' Parker says before I can overanalyse this any more, and I look down to see a bunch of dollars in his hand. 'It's payment for today. Can you be back here at eight a.m. tomorrow? I have to go to work then, but you'll be okay with Dad, won't you?'

It's hard to say no when confronted with cash and, as I take it, I realise there is enough here to buy my own groceries for the next week.

'Erm...'

'Great, I'll see you tomorrow,' Parker says as he heads for the door and then opens it, clearly inviting me to leave now my shift is at an end.

I look at Joe, who is still sleeping, before looking at the money in my hand, and figure it's hardly been the most difficult way to earn a living, so I put the money into my purse and head for the open doorway.

'See you tomorrow,' I say to Parker as I pass him, and he nods. I make my way to the elevator, hearing the apartment door close behind me.

I think about Parker and Joe all the way home as I walk along the beachfront and pass roller skaters, busking musicians and sunset sunbathers. I'm still thinking about them as I reach the door to my apartment, a building a world away from the gleaming high-rises further down the beach, but actually only a fifteen-minute walk. The white paint on the exterior of the building is peeling, and the flimsy gate that acts as security here is nothing like the electronic door to Joe's place, nor are there any of the nice neighbours that man has. Instead of being around smiling pensioners, I'm living in close quarters to shadier types, people I don't trust and people who would prob- ably screw me over if they ever got the chance. That's why I keep a tight grip on my purse as I walk to my apartment door, aware that there's plenty of cash in there and afraid that some- body might try and take it from me. Nobody does, though I don't make it inside without the long-haired man in the next apartment poking his head out of the door and seeing me.

'There she is!' he cries. 'My favourite neighbour! Where have you been all day?'

'At work,' I reply quietly as I unlock my door.

'Then you'll need a drink. Care to come inside and have one with me?'

'No, thank you,' I say as I open my door, but I'm worried my neighbour isn't going to let me go that easily. His name is Ross, or Russell, or something like that. I forget. But whatever it is, it's obvious that he's attracted to me. But while I've tried to make it just as obvious that the feeling is not mutual, he never seems to get the hint, or he simply refuses to give up.

'Are you sure? It could be fun,' he tries one more time, but I apologise before going inside and then lock my door as quickly as I can.

Sighing deeply, I look around my humble home, the one I've lived in for the past three months, and I don't have much to show for my time here. The only furnishings are the things that were here when I moved in – a microwave, a small fridge, an uncomfortable sofa, a bed that's just as bad and a TV with barely any channels on it. But I manage here, mainly because I try to go out a lot, if only for a walk, but also because I spend most of my time looking at one thing. It's the thing I go to get now, and I find it lying under my pillow where I always leave it. It's a small notebook and I open it to see the photos of the people who are apparently my family.

I see a dark-haired woman in her fifties and the name written beside it.

Scarlett.

But it's the word written beside the name that should mean more.

Mom.

Except it doesn't mean more. That's because, despite this photo and this note telling me who this is, I don't actually remember this woman. But then that's the whole point of this notebook. The person who gave it to me told me to look at it every day or I would forget all the people mentioned within it.

The next person is Adrian, and I look at the photo of the man in his fifties with salt-and-pepper hair before my eyes move over the word *Dad*. But again, it's just a photo and words and it's hard to feel the emotion that should be attached to them.

I turn the page and see the person who gave me this notebook. The photo shows a woman of a similar age to me, and she is smiling. Even though I struggle to feel who this person is just the same, there is a little more warmth to her image.

Pippa – Sister.

I know Pippa gave me this notebook, the writing on the next page tells me so, and I read the note like I do every day. It's very important that I do.

Dear Darcy,

You need to read this every single day and do as I say. We are your family, and we love you, but we cannot be with you. You're safer away from here and you will be safe as long as you stay away. Look at our photos every day and make sure you

remember us like we will remember you. But make sure you do
as I say on the next page. It's crucial that you do.

Love you sis,

Pippa

It's the next page that I turn to now, and there are two sentences written in big, bold writing, the two warnings that I am to adhere to and have been adhering to ever since I got here.

NEVER WATCH THE NEWS

NEVER EVER COME BACK HOME

Feeling frustrated like I always do whenever I look at this notebook, I put it back under my pillow and lie down on my bed, wishing I knew why my sister was giving me such warnings. I have a family out there who I apparently cannot visit, but I can't remember why. I'm guessing the news might give me a clue, but Pippa says I can't watch that, and I've followed her advice. She clearly cares for me. I know that because, as well as sending me some money once I told her my new address, she has been writing letters to me to make sure I'm okay. I am able to reply to those letters by sending them to a PO Box in Chicago, so I assume my family is there, but that's all I know. Well, that and the fact that there is one final thing written in small writing on the back page of this notebook.

In case of emergency, if you find this notebook and the person
who owns it is in distress, help her get back here:

1 Sherwood Crescent, Winnetka, Chicago, Illinois

I assume that's my parents' address, or maybe Pippa's.

So what's stopping me from going there? Every single other thing that's written in this notebook for one. There must be a very important reason why I can't go home.

I don't know what it is.

But according to Pippa, it's better that it stays that way.

I am putting my trust in the fact that my family knows best.

FIVE

PIPPA

I run a hand over my tired face and ask myself a question every nurse must ask themselves at least six times a day.

Why am I doing this job?

Like most nurses, I never get to actually answer that question because I'm too busy to have the time required to properly ponder it. Today is no different, and as yet another long shift finishes, I race to my car, catching a glimpse of myself in my vehicle's window and seeing my uniform and my very tired face before I get in behind the wheel and start the engine.

I drive out of the hospital parking lot as quickly but also as carefully as I can, having to adhere to the very slow speed limits that exist here because so many patients and their families are wandering around. But just because I'm driving slowly, it doesn't mean that I'm not in a hurry. Once I'm out of the vicinity of the hospital, the speed limit increases, and I can gradually put my foot down on the gas pedal.

I've got ten minutes to go and pick up my four-year-old son from kindergarten. I'll take him home and feed him before getting him ready for bed. I might have just finished work, but my daily tasks are far from complete. I've also just finished a shift where I spent the entire time providing care for sick children, some of them even younger than my son, but again, that doesn't mean my caring duties for a child are at an end yet. Campbell, the busy, boisterous boy I gave birth to four years ago, is the light of my life, but he's also the most exhausting part of it and, coming from a nurse, that's saying a lot. I love being a mother, but I hate being a tired one. I wish I had more energy so I could savour time with my son more, but as it is, I'm constantly exhausted, forever frazzled, and that means Campbell is not exactly getting the best of me. But I'm not the only one he's not getting the best of. He certainly isn't getting the best from his father, Karl, either and he's not alone there. I'm not getting the best of Karl myself, but unlike my son, I am not tethered to that man forever.

Karl will always be Campbell's dad.

But he doesn't always have to be my husband.

I feel bad. I know I still love him, deep down, where it counts, rather than on the surface, where everything is much more superficial and easier to change. I get evidence of how easy it is to alter the surface of things when I glance at my left hand on the steering wheel, the one without my wedding ring. It's not there because I took it off months ago after a particularly bad fight with my husband, and I haven't put it back on since. We're still together, or at least we're still in the same house and going through the motions of married life, but we're broken, there's no denying that, and it's sadly debatable as to whether we can be fixed at this point.

We have so many happy memories together, the highlights being our sun-kissed wedding in Florida and, of course, welcoming our little boy after an intense and tear-filled labour, but more current situations have knocked us off course. Darcy's accident. My distracted state of mind. His frustration. A collective sense of exhaustion that suffocates us on a daily basis.

Maybe things are salvageable.

Or maybe we don't have the energy for it anymore.

Divorce is hardly the most fun thing for a tired and stressed parent to think about on their way to their next errand, but the word is very prominent in my mind and, unfortunately, has been for some time. My marriage is on the rocks, there's no denying that, just like there's no pretending that it's all the fault of one person. Like any relationship, it takes two, and I guess I'm as much to blame for the cracks between me and Karl as he is.

I could put all of our problems on him getting home from work late every night and not providing me with enough help with our son, or the fact he likes to drink too much when he does get a day off – or any one of a million little things that annoy me about him these days, right down to the way he leaves the toothpaste cap off or only takes the trash out when the bag is at the point of bursting. But it wouldn't be fair of me to say it's all him, because I'm guilty of many things too. My job is demanding like his, meaning I'm overworked too, and I bring a lot of my stresses home with me. Even though I spend more time with Campbell than he does, it's still not as much as I'd like. And while I don't choose to spend my free days drinking, I do spend most of them dealing with my family issues, of which there are many, and that is putting it very mildly.

There's no doubt that things became tougher for me and Karl when my sister, Darcy, had her accident. The car crash that my poor sibling was in over two years ago almost robbed her of her life, and while she survived, it robbed her of something.

Her memory.

Darcy suffers from retrograde amnesia, which means she can remember nothing from before her accident, and also has trouble retaining long-term memories, meaning she is prone to forgetting about things that have occurred after a few weeks have passed. It's been devastating for her, both personally and professionally, but she's not the only one. To say that it has put a strain on our family would be the understatement of the year, because as anybody who has dealt with a loved one and memory loss will know, trying to regularly convince someone you are close to of who you are and who they are is exhausting, upsetting and, sometimes, impossible. But like any family, we don't give up on each other, and I never gave up on my little sister, who has always been far more than just my sibling. She's been my best friend, and I couldn't live with myself if I didn't try and get her back. Nor could our parents, Adrian and Scarlett. The three of us rallied around Darcy and did whatever we could to try and help her regain her memory, or at least try and make her day-to-day life more manageable in her new condition. But that took time, a lot of time, and it was all time that I was spending away from my other family, my husband and son, and as such, problems began to appear there too.

Karl understood that I was struggling with my sister's accident and needed to spend time helping her, but he started to draw the line when I was doing more unorthodox things to help her regain her memory. The best example of that would be when my parents and I decided to role play; I pretended to be Darcy's colleague, while Mom pretended to be a patient and Dad had pretended to be her worried partner. That whole charade took time to plan and implement, and I have to admit that I was not exactly present with Karl or Campbell during that difficult and unusual time. I also had to take precious vacation days to do it, depriving my husband and son of a holiday with me this year, which only added to my partner's frustration. Worst of all, the role-playing didn't really work as we'd hoped, but of course, that wasn't the worst of it. Not really.

The worst thing was what I had to do when a few glimmers of Darcy's memory surprisingly came back to her.

As I sit in traffic and lean my weary head against the wheel as another light turns red, I think about the body I helped to hide. It was the body of a man my sister was once intimately involved with, a man who murdered his sick wife while Darcy was caring for her – this was before Darcy's accident.

Laurence Murphy.

Darcy remembered what happened between her, Laurence and his wife, Melissa, and it was bad. Working as Melissa's nurse as she battled cancer, Darcy became romantically involved with Laurence, which was unprofessional and, I felt, out of character too, but nothing more dangerous than that. But things took a sinister turn when Laurence suggested he and Darcy could be together much sooner if Melissa died ahead of schedule, and he had wanted Darcy to be the one to end his wife's life. Thankfully, Darcy did not kill Melissa. Laurence killed her and, as if that wasn't bad enough, he also embarked on an affair with Darcy's colleague and best friend, Eden. The shock and horror of it all was enough to cause my poor sister to lose control of her car and crash while on the way to report Laurence's crime to the police – and it was that crash which changed all our lives forever. But my life took an even more troubling turn recently, when Darcy recalled those events. She was then in danger with both Laurence and Eden, who were preparing to kill her to silence her forever. Fortunately, my sister survived, but she had to kill Laurence. It was self-defence, she told me. By the time I found her, there was a need for his dead body to be concealed. We could have called the police and told them the truth, but would they have believed a woman with memory loss? I decided we couldn't take that risk, not if it meant my sibling going to jail, or for me and my parents losing her in such a way, so I protected my sister and got rid of Laurence's body. It was incredibly stressful, and I'll never really recover from it, but I couldn't stand by and watch her be arrested. I did what I had to do and then I told Darcy to get out of Chicago. I knew that, thankfully, given time, she would forget all about what we had done.

It sounds awful but I have been able to use my sister's

memory issues to both of our advantage. Darcy forgets things a few weeks after they've occurred unless she is reminded regularly, so I knew she would forget about Laurence and where we had disposed of his body once she left home. But I also knew she would forget us too, which is why I gave her a notebook with our photos in it, as well as some very clear instructions that are designed to prevent her from stumbling back upon the truth, returning home and, ultimately, stumbling right into the middle of a police investigation.

So far, Laurence's body has not been discovered lurking beneath the frigid depths of Lake Michigan, as the temperatures plummet at this time of year, at least for us in the north of the country anyway. But it's much warmer where my sister is down in Florida, where she has started her new life and where I write to her to make sure she is doing okay and not getting into any more problems. I might visit one day, or maybe secretly head down south to observe her from a distance and check she is managing things. But for now, I'm needed more up here as I try and keep another part of my family together.

Needless to say, I haven't told my husband about any of what happened with Darcy. He does not need to know what my sister and I have done, mainly because I can't trust that he won't go to the police. Not even my parents know about the body. It's mine and my sister's secret; yet really, I'm the only one burdened by it because, unlike my sibling, my memory is entirely intact.

Such is the cross I must bear to keep my sister safe.

That all explains why I've hardly been wife of the year to Karl, or the most present mother to Campbell, but I am trying, just like I'm trying to get through this traffic jam as quickly as possible so I can collect my son on time. But it's not easy, none of it is, and I don't know how things are going to go in the future.

I'm fighting for my marriage; I'm fighting to hold down my

demanding job while juggling parenthood; and, most of all, I'm fighting the paranoia that comes with spending every day wondering if the police are ever going to uncover our crimes and send me and Darcy to prison for the rest of our lives.

Is that enough for a working, married mom to have to deal with?

If not, there's also the issue of my parents.

Adrian and Scarlett don't know why Darcy had to leave Chicago so suddenly three months ago, just that it had something to do with me because I'm the one who drove her to the bus station. That means they blame me for Darcy not being around anymore, which only makes my life even more difficult. It's a crazy situation to have put myself in, and I'm terrified saving Darcy is going to cost me everybody else I love, but I've done it and there's no going back now.

As I'm stuck in traffic, I see Dad is trying to call me, but I don't pick up, not only because it's illegal to use my phone while at the wheel but because I can't face talking to him right now. He's probably going to tell me how upset Mom still is, or how he doesn't understand why Darcy and I have been shutting them out. I've had that conversation before and I'm sure I'll have that conversation many times again, but not today.

Today, I need to focus on one thing at a time and my next stop is kindergarten to get my gorgeous boy.

But as I drive on, I think about how I would feel if Campbell suddenly left, and I had no idea why or where he was going. I'd surely be as confused and distressed as my parents are about Darcy, so I can understand their pain.

Oh sis, you've really left a mess for me to sort out here.

I just hope your new life is better than the one you've left behind.

Surely it can't be any worse...

SIX

DARCY

I've spent most of my evening writing a letter to Pippa to update her on my situation, and it seems a good time to write because I have news. I've told her all about my new job caring for Joe and how my first day went and, while I feel out of my depth acting as a nurse sometimes, I also feel strangely drawn to doing it, like it's what I was born to do and I'm just a little out of practice.

Not for the first time, I've included a few questions in my letter to my sister as well, questions that she has skipped over or plainly ignored so far when she has written back, but questions that I will always keep asking until I get some answers.

Questions like: what did I do for a job before? What were my hobbies and interests?

Basically, I want to figure out what my purpose is in life.

However, I'm guessing the reason Pippa has never written back to tell me about those things means they must be connected to whatever shady past I have and the things I got involved with that have forced me to leave Chicago. Surely, if there was no issue, then she would just tell me. As it is, I'm forced to stumble on by myself and try and figure out what is best for me without a real guide, as if I'm flying a plane with no coordinates and somehow expecting to magically land where I need to be.

I plan to post this latest letter to my sister on my way to work tomorrow morning, which will be a simple enough task, but before that I need to tackle a much more difficult one.

I need to get to sleep.

It's early evening and I can still see some sunlight coming in from outside, as well as hear a few bursts of laughter coming from people having fun at the beach. But they aren't the main reasons why I might struggle to get some rest for a while.

It might be an everyday thing that most people don't even think about, but for me sleep is always an incredible hurdle to overcome. I cannot shut my brain off when I lay my head down on the pillow, and I know I need to do something about it. Sleeping pills, anxiety meds, whatever might help make this process smoother would be worth trying. But getting access to those would require going to a doctor and I haven't done that yet, mainly because any good doctor would most likely ask me about my medical history before prescribing any drugs, and that's a total black hole to me. All I know about my past is in the notebook under my spare pillow beside me, but I can hardly offer that up to a doctor for them to read. They'll simply look at me with a confused expression and ask me if it's some kind of a joke.

Except I wouldn't be laughing.

I'd probably cry like I'm on the verge of doing right now.

I can feel a few tears running down my face and onto my pillow, and I try and wipe them away as quickly as possible – that seems better than letting them flow freely and dampening my mood as well as my pillow even further. I try to tell myself that, as bad as I might feel I have it now, there are always people who are worse off than me in the world and I should be grateful for what I've got. Like Joe, for example. That poor man is losing control of his mind, and while I have only witnessed the minor problems it brings for him so far, like using his phone to try and turn the volume up on the television, I know there are far worse aspects to it than that. I know because Parker told me about some of those; like Joe accusing Parker of killing his mom.

That must be an awful thing for a son to have to hear from his father. Parker would be grieving for the loss of his mom anyway without having his dad say it was all his fault. But Joe is just confused, losing his grip on reality more and more every day, and soon, he probably won't even remember who his son is, never mind what he thinks he might have done.

As I think about it, I'm struck by the similarities between me and the patient I'm now being paid to look after. We're both forgetting things, getting confused, and most of all I guess we're both afraid. Afraid of the future. Afraid of what might happen if we don't get better.

Although there is a big difference between me and Joe. He's actually been diagnosed with a medical condition, of which there is a prognosis and pathway to navigate it. I haven't – or not that I know of. I don't know what is going on with me, only that Pippa, this person who says she is my sister, wants me to avoid the news and avoid going home.

Am I dangerous?

Are the police looking for me?

Am I a killer?

It seems totally bizarre to think that I could be: look at the state of me. I'm curled up in the foetal position in my bed, alone, shedding tears and feeling very vulnerable, so it's ludicrous to think that I could be some kind of menace to society. It's better to tell myself that the reason for my current situation is perhaps not to keep others safe but to keep *me* safe. Maybe there is somebody out there looking to hurt me, somebody from the past who I cannot remember.

Who knows? It's just another night of lying awake and

questioning my life. I put up with it for a couple more hours before, mercifully, I achieve sleep.

Any thoughts that such a thing might give me peace of mind are laughable because no sooner have I slipped into a slumber than I have one of my weird dreams again. As usual, I see the same two people I always see.

I see *her*, the poorly patient lying in bed and begging me for help.

Then I see *him*, the handsome man standing beside me, letting me know that everything is going to be okay and that things will be better when this woman before us has gone.

I've seen these people in my dreams for a while now, though I don't know who they are. But this dream takes a sinister turn when the scene suddenly changes and it's the man who is the one begging for his life. He's on the floor and I'm standing over him – when I look down, I see that I am holding a syringe.

What has happened? Have I injected him with something?

Am I the reason he seems to be dying?

The natural thing would be to help him, but I don't do that, as if a part of me knows that it's better this way, if I just leave him to gasp for breath until he stops. And he does stop, the life eventually leaving him. Now he's still.

This is simply a bad dream, the dream version of me says before I urge myself to wake up. I'll feel better when I do. I'll realise this dream was nonsense and then I can go back to sleep and start a new dream, a nicer one, or better yet, have no dream at all. But I can't force myself to wake up and the longer I'm stuck here with this man's body, the worse I feel.

Until somebody asks me what I've just done.

The syringe falls from my hand as I turn around and see Pippa standing there. What is my sister doing here in this dream world? It looks like she's here to help me. She tells me she can take care of all of this, but I'm going to have to trust her.

So I do.

Then I wake up.

I'm sweating, even though I can see the sun has gone down outside now, and my heart is racing, even though I've been doing nothing more strenuous than lying in bed. It must be because my brain has clearly told my body that the dream I had might be more than that.

It might have been a memory.

I'm wide awake now, so give up on sleep and pick up the notebook again, turning to the page with Pippa's photo. Yep, this is definitely the same person I saw in my dream. But who was that man? I have no way to find out if I don't have a name for him.

Unless...

I think about checking the news. What if I don't see him and get no answers? Or worse, what if I do see him and it's bad? Really, really bad.

I close my eyes before I can be tempted for a second longer to look at the news.

Follow the advice in the book.

Heed the warnings.

It must be better for me if I don't know what I'm really capable of.

SEVEN

PIPPA

'No, don't touch that!'

I dive at my son before he can put his hand anywhere near the burning hot stove where I'm busy making his evening meal, and I manage to prevent the disaster that would have occurred if his skin had come into contact with the searing surface above him.

Campbell isn't happy that I've stopped him from doing something he wanted to do, but I'm relieved. He'd be in tears now, crying his little eyes out, and like any loving parent, I can't bear to see my child in pain. If the worst had happened, I'd also be preparing to spend the evening at the hospital waiting frantically for somebody to treat his burns. Finding myself stressing in a hospital is the last place I want to be given that I work in one all day, and I'll be back in one tomorrow once I've got through another hectic night at home.

'Go and play with your toys and I'll bring your food to you when it's ready,' I suggest to my temperamental child, who after only four years of life has surely already shaved several years off my own, such is the amount of stress he likes to put me under. I love him more than anything, but that doesn't mean he's not exhausting and, not for the first time since I've been home, I glance at the clock and wonder when reinforcements will be on the way.

Karl was due back from work almost an hour ago, but this isn't the first time my husband has been late recently. The more problems that the pair of us have had in our marriage, the longer he seems to spend at the office, which is clearly an avoidance tactic and one that I don't appreciate. It's also one that I wouldn't even consider using myself. Who would collect Campbell from kindergarten or get him home and entertain him and make his dinner and get him ready for bed and so on? Karl used to be a much more hands-on parent, taking Campbell to the park and organising picnics for all three of us, but lately it's as if he's detaching himself from his family duties, although he'll only say I was doing the same thing a few months ago when I was spending all my time dealing with Darcy and her problems. I told him that was different, I was helping my family, but he says it was to the detriment of the family we have, and we've never really recovered from that, even with Darcy out of the picture now.

But it's not as if Karl hasn't given me any opportunity to revert back to his previously more helpful ways. He says he'll be a better husband when I start being a better wife, and what he means by that is he's waiting for me to stop keeping secrets from him and start telling him the truth. He knows something bad happened with my sister and he wants me to tell him what it is. He's right about one thing. Something very bad did happen, but he's wrong if he thinks I'll ever reveal it – hence our problem.

He says the trust has gone from our marriage and maybe it has, a fact that is more my fault than his.

But how am I supposed to tell him that my sister killed a man?

Even more than that, how I am supposed to say that I helped her to dispose of his body?

I'm pleased when Campbell does as I say and goes to play with his toys, and I'm also pleased when I hear the front door open a few minutes later, because it means Karl is home and I have some back-up to help with bedtime shortly. But the tension in this house has just gone up by several notches now that my husband is here, and I prepare to spend the upcoming few hours trying to navigate our marital troubles as well as all the other ones I have. How I wish we could go back to when Campbell was born and the three of us existed in a bubble of bliss. That bubble has been popped now and, as a consequence, all three of us seem to be getting further away from each other.

'How was your day?' I ask Karl as he enters the kitchen, but he shrugs before grabbing a beer from the fridge.

'Campbell okay?' he asks me as he twists the cap open and takes a swig, while making a visual check on what stage I'm up to with dinner.

'Yeah, but I think he'd like a little playtime with his daddy,' I suggest, hoping my husband is receptive to it. Thankfully, he is. As Karl goes to find our son, I tell him I'll bring our food in shortly.

This night could be going worse, I think to myself, comparing it to recent evenings when Karl hasn't even acknowledged me, when I've eaten my dinner alone while he's been upstairs continuing to avoid me.

As I finish the cooking and turn off the hot stove that Campbell almost burnt himself on, I'm thinking everything is going okay. But then I hear my phone ringing, and when I see it's Dad calling, I realise I still haven't returned any of his missed calls.

He's really keen to talk to me about something, whatever it may be, and I feel bad for not answering, but I have enough going on here at the moment. It can't be that important or he'd send me a text message or come and see me directly.

He knows exactly where I am.

It's his other daughter he has no idea about.

I decide not to answer this latest call. I can't afford to spend too long chatting on the phone. I certainly don't want to take away time I could be spending with Karl and Campbell, because doing that is what's put such a strain on us in the first place, so I'll leave it and try Dad later perhaps, when my son is in bed and my husband is in the shower.

I turn my phone to silent then serve up the food before expertly carrying three plates into the playroom, where I find Karl sitting on the floor with Campbell and a large train set parked in between them.

'Are we eating in here?' Karl asks, and I shrug, saying it should be fine as it's only pasta, and even Campbell can't make that much of a mess with it. Our son takes a seat at his miniature table and chair set while Karl and I sit on the floor, surrounded by toys, but I don't care because this is all I need right now.

My family, together, and, for the time being, at peace.

That peace is threatened when Campbell asks if we can watch TV while we eat and, as Karl grabs the remote and starts flicking through the channels, I feel a knot tightening in my stomach. I get this exact feeling every time the TV goes on, as well as the radio in the car, or whenever I see the front page of a newspaper as I pass the shelves in the supermarket. The reason for the stomach-churning sensation whenever I'm confronted by any form of media is because I'm terrified what the news might have to say if I see or hear it.

Like anybody who has done something they shouldn't have, I live in constant fear of being caught and that's why, whenever I'm susceptible to a news update, I'm afraid that I'm going to learn that the body I dumped in Lake Michigan has been found.

'Just put some cartoons on,' I say to my husband as he absentmindedly scrolls through the channels, and while it sounds like I'm choosing something our son might like to watch, it's really because I want him to stop before he happens across the news. If he does that, I might hear a reporter saying something very frightening and, if I do, I won't be able to control my reaction. Thankfully, Karl finds some cartoons and Campbell is happy to watch them, so I can relax, though only temporarily. I know that trying to avoid the news forever is not healthy or even wise, but it's better if I check it when I'm alone and can manage the situation better. If the news ever does come through that Laurence's body has been discovered, I have no doubt that I'll enter into a full-blown panic attack, but it's not so bad if I'm by myself when that happens. Heaven forbid it occurs around my son, who will be scared to witness such a thing, or worse, my husband, who would surely figure out that I had something to do with that body if I was losing my mind over it.

I wrote in Darcy's notebook that she was to avoid watching the news because I didn't want it stirring up any memories for her, but I'm just as afraid of it as she is and I guess that fear will never go away.

Let's hope I make it through the rest of my life without Laurence's body being found. But realistically, is that going to happen?

I'm afraid my life's not that perfect.

I know it's only a matter of time until somebody finds that body. We hid him in a rush, at nighttime, in an ever-changing lake beside one of the busiest cities in the country.

When they do, it'll make all my current problems seem laughable in comparison.

EIGHT

DARCY

I wake after a restless night with my soul still unsettled by that bad dream I had, so I spend the first minutes of my day looking at the notebook like I usually do before I get up and prepare for work. I'm getting ready to go to look after Joe again, and Parker needs me to be on time today as he has work to go to, so I don't want to disappoint him. I leave my place promptly and only stop once on the way to post the letter I wrote for Pippa last night.

The beach is empty as I walk along it, though I see a few empty bottles scattered around on the sand, no doubt left behind by a few of the revellers whose voices I could hear while I was lying in bed alone. I guess they all had fun out here, socialising, making memories – basically doing things that aren't part of my own life anymore.

I make it to Joe's apartment ten minutes early and try the buzzer. The door opens quickly, the sound of Parker's voice over the intercom letting me know he's grateful that I'm prompt. I wonder what time Parker gets here in the morning to make sure his dad is okay to start the day, but it must be exhausting, and it's no wonder he needs another pair of hands to juggle things.

As I travel up in the elevator, my thoughts shift from feeling sympathetic towards my employer to wondering if he has anything to hide, like Joe mentioned yesterday, but by the time I knock on the door, my only thoughts are about getting through today so I can be given another handful of dollars.

'Hey, Darcy. Good to see you,' Parker says, looking weary but still handsome, and also not looking like he's dressed for work today, unless there is a very lax dress code at his work-place. I was expecting him to be wearing a shirt and tie or at least something reasonably smart, but here he is in shorts, a vest and sneakers, looking like he's going for a run rather than going to be a good employee. But then again, this is Florida, where the dress code is casual and it's impossible sometimes to tell between a guy going to work and a guy going to the beach, so maybe he simply doesn't have to be too smart for his boss. His casual appearance certainly hasn't diminished his attractive-ness, not that I should dwell on that given his partner and all.

'Everything okay?' I ask as I enter Joe's apartment and look around for the homeowner, but I don't see him.

'Not really. Joe's still in bed. I tried to get him up, but he's refusing.'

'Oh. Maybe he's tired.'

'No, he's depressed, though he won't admit it.'

'Depressed?'

'Yeah. Wouldn't you be if a doctor said you were losing your memory?'

I don't need a doctor to tell me my memory isn't right – I only have to try and think of anything more than a couple of weeks ago to realise there is a black hole there, but I nod sympa-thetically.

'How about I go and see him, and you get yourself off to work,' I suggest, and Parker appreciates that.

'Thanks. Good luck today. I hope you don't need it.'

He grabs an apple before leaving.

Once I'm alone, I stare at the closed bedroom door and wonder how long I should leave it before going in there. It might be easier for me to stay out here for as long as possible, but that wouldn't really be doing my job, would it?

'Joe?' I call out as I knock on the door before entering the bedroom, though I quickly wish I hadn't when I find the man standing beside his bed wearing nothing but a wide grin.

'Oh, my goodness! I'm sorry!' I say, quickly putting a hand over my eyes and wishing I hadn't just seen what I saw, but Joe doesn't seem too bothered by it, which makes me think he might have planned it. But it's hard to be angry at a man with his condition. I'm not sure what is on purpose and what is as a result of his confusion, so I ask him to get dressed before leaving the bedroom and waiting for him in the kitchen.

Joe emerges ten minutes later, fully clothed, and doesn't seem at all bothered by what happened, simply opening a set of sliding doors and stepping out onto the balcony that overlooks the beach. He might just be getting some fresh air, but I have a moment of panic that he's about to topple over the railing and fall to his death, so I rush out to join him before he can get too close to the edge. I'm guessing Parker asked me to watch out for his father for moments exactly like this one. There's no doubt that a high-rise apartment can be a dangerous place for a person like Joe.

'Beautiful morning, Maggie,' he says to me once I'm beside him, as he breathes in the fresh air, his hands on the stainless-steel railing.

'I'm sorry?' I reply, unsure what he called me.

'What time are you meeting your friends for lunch today?' Joe asks me, still not looking at me but at the magnificent view below.

I realise that Joe has got me mixed up with somebody else

and, a few seconds later, I figure Maggie must be his late wife. I guess it was a habit of his to come out here when he woke up and chat to his wife, but now she's gone and he's ill, he thinks she's me. His brain must be operating out of habit, but what should I do about it?

'I'm Darcy,' I remind him gently, hoping I won't upset him too much when he realises his mistake, but figuring it's best to correct him rather than have to spend all day pretending to be someone I'm not.

'Yes, I know that. I'm not a fool,' Joe snaps at me, and now I'm the one who is confused, though he quickly makes me see sense. 'I was talking to her spirit, not to you. She always had lunch with the girls on a Tuesday, so as it's a Tuesday today, I was having a chat with her.'

'I'm sorry. I didn't realise,' I say, feeling really bad now to ruin this man's moment with his late wife, but Joe just shakes his head then goes back inside, leaving me languishing on the balcony and feeling like my presence here is making things worse rather than better.

I spend the next few hours with Joe, engaging in some interesting conversations about his time spent as a travelling salesman in the seventies and eighties, where his memory seems surprisingly sharp as he recounts his tales from the road. But then there are sad reminders of the reality of his situation, like when he shouts at somebody on the television as if they are supposed to be able to hear him, or when he tells me that he enjoyed Christmas last week, despite that particular holiday being a few months away yet. I also have to remind him who I am, as well as explain to him where his son is, and I have to do that several times. Not that I mind because this is part of the job. But I'd be lying if I said it wasn't a relief when Joe tells me a baseball game is starting and he wants to watch it. I know that will keep him occupied now for the next few hours.

It certainly does, and by the time the game has finished, a

game that I struggled to keep my eyes open through because I found it so boring, I notice Joe has fallen asleep. I turn the volume down on the TV and take the opportunity to tidy up our lunch plates in the kitchen before returning to the sofa. But when I do, I see something that sends a shiver through my body.

A TV news bulletin is starting.

It's silly for such a thing to make me nervous, but Pippa's warning in my notebook immediately comes to mind, so I reach for the remote control to either change the channel or turn the television off entirely. But just before I can do either of those things, Joe wakes up.

'Leave it. I want to watch this,' he says, and he takes the remote from me before I can do anything else with it.

I realise that the news is staying on now, whether I like it or not, but that's not good. I shouldn't be watching this, should I?

'Is there anything else we could watch?' I ask hopefully, but Joe ignores me and turns the volume up to show what he thinks of that idea. As I stare at the screen, I see that this is a national news bulletin. The first report is about a drugs scandal in New York.

I tell myself again I should stop watching. I could go in the kitchen and pretend to be busy there, or simply go to the bathroom and come back when the news is mostly over. But I find it impossible to tear myself away from watching it now; it's as if I have denied myself of this one thing and, now that it's forbidden, I just can't resist having access to it.

I keep watching the TV nervously, though I've no idea what I'm expecting to see or if I'll even know what it is if I see it, and the reports keep coming. A flood in Houston. A fight at a mall in Minnesota. Nothing is troubling me any more than it should though. Nothing is giving me any reason to understand why Pippa has told me to not watch the news ever again. Then the reporter starts talking about Chicago, and simply hearing the name of the city where I presume my family is makes me sit up a little straighter and hold my breath.

'Detectives involved in the search for Laurence Murphy and Eden Carthy are again appealing to the public for help,' the reporter says as the feed cuts to a shot of a house on a street. 'In particular, they are seeking to identify the two women who were seen on the street where the missing couple lived, in the early hours of the morning around the time of their disappearance. Those women are persons of interest but, as of yet, have not been located. It's now been three months since Laurence Murphy and Eden Carthy went missing and many questions remain about their whereabouts.'

That's when two photos appear on screen and, when they do, I let out an audible gasp, one that causes Joe to look at me and frown.

'What is it?' he asks me, but I don't answer him. One, because I'm too shocked to speak, and two, because I dare not say a word even if I could. That's because I recognise one of the people on the news. Now I know why Pippa told me to avoid watching these programmes at all costs.

I know the man this news report is about.

Laurence Murphy.

He's the man from my dreams – or should I say my nightmares.

He's the one who was dying as I stood over him with a syringe in my hand.

So I guess he's the reason I can never go home again.

NINE

PIPPA

Another manic morning has meant that it's almost midday
before I realise what I forgot to do last night. I forgot to call Dad
and see what he was trying to speak to me about.

'Can you cover for me? I really need to make a call,' I ask
one of my colleagues on the ward and, thankfully, she says yes,
probably because we're enjoying a brief lull in the usual chaos,
so I can spare a few minutes away.

I don't make a habit of sneaking off shift to make a personal
call, but I feel terrible for not ringing Dad sooner. I meant to do
it last night after dinner but, as tends to happen, the evening
just got away from me. After sitting through a stressful news
bulletin that scrambled my brain as I tried not to imagine the
reporter telling the viewers that a body had been found in Lake
Michigan and the police were already on their way to a
suspect's house, I had gone straight into getting Campbell ready
for bed. Some nights it can be fairly quick, but last night he
wanted extra bedtime stories and he wanted me to be the one to
read them, not his father. I couldn't be mad at my son for
wanting me to sit with him as he wound down from another
busy day. I certainly know the years will fly by and I'll miss

nights like that with him, but last night I really could have done without the extra strain on my time. As it was, I did the best I could as a mother, reading and reading until Campbell closed his eyes and drifted off to sleep.

By the time I emerged from his bedroom, I was more than ready to go into my own. Karl was already set up in the spare bedroom and didn't seem particularly interested in spending as much time with me before going to sleep as our son did, so I left him to it in there and got in my own bed, alone. Then, completely forgetting about all the missed calls from Dad because I was so exhausted, I turned off the light and went to sleep, not waking until dawn, when Campbell crept in and said he was hungry.

I got him fed and ready for kindergarten, then I was in the car on the way to work, and now it's suddenly lunchtime and I'm finally returning Dad's calls.

I really hope it was nothing serious.

'Come on, pick up the phone,' I mutter under my breath while standing around the back of the hospital, in a part where staff members can loiter and make quick phone calls before turning off our personal devices and going back inside to where the patients are. Annoyingly, Dad isn't answering now, possibly because he is busy doing something else, but potentially because he's mad at me for ignoring him for so long and this is now some kind of payback. Not to be fully deterred, I decide to call Mom to see if I can get through to him that way, and she does answer my call, although I almost wish she hadn't when I hear her weary voice at the other end of the line.

'What do you want?' Mom asks me with all the usual vigour she reserves for her least favourite daughter these days, but I'm seasoned enough to roll with it without it knocking me off my stride.

'Hi. I was just hoping to speak to Dad. He's been calling me. Is he there?'

'Oh, so you've decided to return his calls now. That's nice of you.'

'Mom, please, I don't want another argument.'

'You should have thought about that before you took your sister away from us and didn't tell us where she went.'

I already knew Mom would be annoyed at me, which is why I would have preferred it if Dad had answered himself, but I guess, like most parents, they come as a package – it's hard to talk to one without the other getting in the way. But what I didn't know when I made this call was whether or not Mom would have started drinking yet today, although now I've heard her voice, I can tell that she has, which is disappointing but not totally surprising. Wine has become my mother Scarlett's best friend since Darcy moved away and I refused to tell her where she'd gone, and a little morning drink or two isn't completely out of character for my mother these days.

'Please can I speak to Dad?' I ask politely, not having the energy to prolong this conversation any longer.

'No, you can't. Not unless he answers his phone to you, anyway,' Mom replies rather curtly.

'What does that mean?'

'It means I can't help you because he's not here.'

'Where is he?' I ask, growing more frustrated by the second.

Why can parents be so difficult? Then again, they'd probably say the same about their children.

'He's at the other house,' Mom says, so at least now I know where he is, the 'other house' being the first family home we had before my parents got rich and bought their second, current and much larger property, in Winnetka, where so many wealthy Chicagoans live.

'What's he doing there?'

'He's packing.'

'What?' I snap back – that was not what I expected to hear, nor what I wanted to hear.

'This is what he was trying to call you about,' Mom goes on before she pauses, and I swear she takes a sip of something before speaking again. 'He's decided to sell our old house. It's full of memories of Darcy and it's making him sad, so he wants to get rid of it.'

'He's selling the house?' I cry, thinking how this is very bad news. 'And you're letting him?'

'Yes, because it's making me sad too. Now Darcy's gone, there's no point having it sitting empty, so we might as well get rid of it.'

This sounds like a snap decision, but knowing my parents as well as I do, there's no way they'd simply choose to sell a house that they hope Darcy might one day return to live in. No, they're clearly bringing this up to punish me and make me feel bad about not telling them where my sister is.

'Just leave it. You don't need the money,' I say, as if that could persuade them to change their minds.

'No, but we need closure, and if Darcy is gone then getting rid of that house will help us move on,' Mom retorts, seemingly willing to hurt herself in getting rid of this house if it hurts me at the same time.

'Dad's at the house right now?' I ask for clarity, because I can't be confident of how reliable an informant Mom is in her current state.

'Yes,' she replies, and that's all I need to know to realise that I'm not going to be able to return to work in a few minutes.

What I need to do is get in my car and get to that house as quickly as possible.

Before Dad finds anything he shouldn't.

Specifically, anything that might give him clues as to why Darcy had to leave so quickly.

TEN

I made an excuse about Campbell being ill and needing to be collected from kindergarten as quickly as possible, and then I raced to my car and sped away from the hospital in the direction of my old family home. It's the one where Darcy and I spent several happy years growing up before we all moved to Winnetka, but more importantly, it's the home that Darcy moved back into after her accident. She lived there while she was recovering, and while we were hoping her memory might return. We had the idea that putting her in a place full of childhood memories would stir up those lost memories inside her head. But it didn't work, not that it was a total waste of time. At least my sister had a safe place to rest and recuperate, one that the whole family had easy access to so we could regularly check on her, but that also came with its problems once I started to realise that my sister had a troubled past.

As soon as I found out what had happened between my sister and Laurence, not to mention Laurence's late wife, Melissa, and Eden, Darcy's ex-colleague and best friend, I had gone into protection mode to make sure my sister was safe. That meant getting her out of Chicago in case the police ever found out. But that protection mode had not ended once my sister was clear of the city. It had continued in the form of searching our old house for anything that my sister might have left behind that could give clues or hints as to her past involvement with those people. I knew she had a diary from before her accident, and while there was nothing incriminating in there, I threw that away, along with everything else she had like her old nurse's uniform and any old photos of her with Eden and other colleagues. Mom and Dad still don't know I did that, and I'm sure they'll be very upset when they discover what I've done. I'm guessing Dad is going to find out very soon if he is in the process of clearing out the house.

The thought of him rummaging through all the boxes in the attic fills me with such dread that it has led to me speeding across the city to get to the house before he can find anything awful. I think I checked everything and made sure there was nothing bad left behind, but what if I missed something? More specifically, what if Darcy had hidden things in places that I couldn't find but my dad might?

At the forefront of my mind are the missing pages from Darcy's diary. The diary seemed to abruptly end on a certain date not long before her fateful car accident, and it was obvious that all the pages after that had been ripped out. It hinted that the thoughts Darcy was recording in the days before her accident were dark, troubling and, potentially, pointing to something illegal. The problem is, I have absolutely no idea where those pages are. I searched the entire house from top to bottom in the hopes that I might find them so I could burn them too, but no luck. All I can hope is that Darcy herself destroyed them before her accident, so they are gone forever. I really hope they're not still in that house somewhere, in the same way I really hope there isn't anything else that could link my sister to bad things that have happened in this city.

But what if there's something I missed?

And what if Dad finds it?

I press my foot down on the gas pedal and speed through a light that had only just turned red, meaning I've probably got away with it, but I'm pushing my luck by driving like this. I could easily attract the attention of a police officer if any patrol cars are out here too. I have no choice. I have to get to the house as quickly as I can, so I can see what stage Dad is up to with the packing and make sure I supervise the rest of it, in case he happens across anything concerning.

As I continue to drive a little faster than the road limits allow, I am cursing myself for not answering Dad's calls sooner. If I had, I could have avoided this panic, because he wouldn't have even started the packing. Maybe I could have convinced him that selling the house was a bad idea and he might not have started at all. At worst, I would have got a heads-up that he was going to the house today, so I could have gone there last night and done one final check to make sure everything was fine. I didn't answer his calls. I was too busy with my own life. Too preoccupied with my own problems to think of someone else's.

Maybe Mom is right.

Maybe I am a terrible daughter.

That thought is rattling around my head as I reach the house and see Dad's car parked outside. I park my vehicle next to his before running to the front door, the same door I would run to as a little girl after I had got off the school bus with Darcy, the pair of us desperate to get inside and get some after-school snacks before turning the TV on and watching all our favourite shows.

Oh, to go back to those simpler times with my sibling, when we would sit on the carpet and stare at that screen, our mouths full of snacks and our hearts full of sibling love. I bet our parents wish they could go back to then too. Before Dad made all his money and moved us across the city. Before Darcy had her accident. Before I helped her hide a dead body.

We were just a normal family then.

We're anything but that now.

'Dad!' I call out as soon as I enter the house, but there's no reply. However, I do see several boxes sitting by the stairs, all of them taped up, proving that he's been productive since he got here.

'Dad? Where are you?' I try again, but there's still no answer, so I start a sweep of the ground floor, checking in every room down here, expecting to find him taping up another box or kneeling over an open one and putting things inside. If I find him like that, patiently packing, I'll breathe a sigh of relief because it'll probably mean he hasn't found anything untoward during the process. What I do not want to see is him staring at something with a perplexed look on his face, or worse, with an expression of horror.

'Dad! Where are you!' I cry, exasperated because he isn't answering me and, having established that he's not downstairs, I look out of the window into the back garden, wondering if he might be out there. But he's not. The garden furniture is still untouched. He hasn't packed that yet.

That must mean he's upstairs.

'Dad?' I shout as I run up the staircase, taking the steps two or even three at a time in some cases, which causes my heart to race even faster than it was while I was driving over here. But he's still not answering me. Is he being deliberately stubborn because I didn't return his calls sooner? Or is there a simpler explanation? Maybe he's not in the house. He could be next door, chatting to a neighbour, telling them about his plans to put this house on the market. That would be a courteous thing to do, and Dad is very courteous, so maybe I am reading far too much into the lack of response I'm getting from him. But then I reach the door to the bedroom that Darcy was sleeping in before she left, and when I open it I solve the mystery of where my father is. He's in here, which means he has been ignoring my calls. When I spot him, I see why.

He is sitting on the rug, but half of it has been lifted up and there are several exposed floorboards beside him. There's also a hole in those floorboards, but that's not the most shocking thing I see. That would be what my dad is holding in his shaking hands, and what I presume he found in that hole in the floor.

They are crumpled pieces of paper and, as I take a step closer, I see exactly what they are.

Darcy's missing diary entries.

ELEVEN

DARCY

'I have to go,' I say to Joe once I emerge from his bathroom, the one I've just been hiding in for the last fifteen minutes. I've been in there ever since I saw the news report featuring the man from my bad dreams, a man who the Chicago police classify as 'missing, presumed dead'.

'What?' Joe asks. 'You're supposed to stay here with me until my son gets home.'

'I know, and I'm really sorry, but something has come up and I need to leave,' I say, which is kind of the truth. Something has come up, although not something external, in my private life, but something that happened right here, thanks to that television and the news report that I really knew I shouldn't have been watching. I have to go immediately – I'm not in any state to function properly as Joe's nurse; not after what I have just seen.

While I now know why Pippa wrote me a clear message in my notebook to never watch the news, I also know enough that I can't just carry on with my day as normal, and that means I cannot be here to look after Joe. I need to go back to my flat and process this information. Try and figure out what it means. See if there is any way this isn't the bad news it seems to be.

'I'm so sorry. I'll call Parker now and tell him I have to leave, and he might be able to come over,' I suggest, taking out my phone, but Joe gets out of his armchair and dismisses that idea.

'No, he's busy. He's paying you to be here, so he doesn't have to be.'

'I know, and I'm terribly sorry, but I have to go,' I repeat, on the verge of tears again – these are new tears, I already shed a few in the bathroom, which is why I went hiding in there for so long after that news bulletin was broadcast. But I couldn't let Joe see how upset I was. He would have asked me questions, more questions than he's already asking me now, so at least I avoided those. Although the longer I remain here, the more chance there is of him figuring out that my desperation to leave has something to do with that report on the missing man in Chicago, because that's when all my distress began.

'I'm so sorry,' I say as I rush to the door, my phone to my ear as I call Parker. I hope he picks up so I can give him my excuses and let him know that his father is going to be unaccompanied. But he doesn't answer and as Joe follows me out into the corridor, I don't know what to do. I need to get out of here and sort out my thoughts, but can I leave this elderly man alone? What if he hurts himself? I'd get the blame, plus I'd never forgive myself, so maybe I should stay. But then I see the door of the apartment next to Joe's opening, and when a woman my age emerges, I sense an opportunity.

'Hello. I'm really sorry to have to ask you this, but could you possibly do me a favour? Could you sit with this man here for a few hours until his son gets home? It's your neighbour. He's called Joe. You might already know him. Would that be okay?'

The poor woman I've just bombarded with questions looks as perplexed as anyone in her position would, and when Joe catches up to me and speaks, she only looks more confused.

'You need to come back inside and do what you are being paid to do,' Joe tells me firmly, 'or my son will fire you and hire someone else.'

The woman looks at him then back to me, but I try her one more time.

'Please. Could you help me?' I ask, but she shakes her head.

'I'm not going to help Parker,' she says. 'I made that mistake once before, but never again.'

With that, the woman walks away and gets into the elevator, leaving me with more questions. But Joe speaks before I have time to ask her what she meant.

'Let's go inside and talk,' he says. 'If you're not bothered about losing your job, fine. But you might be bothered about me telling someone about that missing man on the news who has got you so worked up.'

Joe re-enters his apartment, and I watch him go, in horror, fully aware that he has made the connection between that news bulletin and my distress. I better give him an explanation, any explanation, or he could pass this information on to his son, or worse, the police. That's why I follow him back into his apartment and close the door so none of the other neighbours might hear what we are about to discuss.

'I don't know what you're talking about,' I try lamely, but it's worth a shot. 'What missing man on the news?'

'I might be losing my mind, but it's not totally gone yet,' Joe says with a snigger as he opens a few kitchen cupboards, though I'm not sure why. 'Who is that missing guy and how do you know him?'

'I don't know,' I reply.

Joe finds what he's looking for, which is a bottle of whiskey that looks to have been well hidden at the back of a cupboard, presumably so Parker couldn't find it and remove it.

'Is that a good idea?' I ask Joe as I watch him unscrew the lid and pour himself a strong measure into a crystal glass.

'If you're wondering if the doctors told me to stop drinking then yes, they did. But being sober won't cure me, so I might as well enjoy myself before things get really bad,' Joe replies. He carries his very full glass out onto the balcony and takes a seat there.

I still just want to run from here and go home to figure out why my dreams feature that man on the news, but I'm not sure if it's a good idea leaving a fragile man to drink alone on a balcony, so I go and join him, taking a seat but refusing a drink of my own.

'Did you stay because you're supposed to be looking after me or because I might be onto your secret?' Joe asks calmly as the pair of us look out over the ocean and, if he's anything like me, he's wishing he was as carefree as some of the people splashing around down there.

'I don't have a secret,' I reply, longing to be as calm as the turquoise water below us.

'Wow, you must be the only person in the world who doesn't,' Joe replies with a chuckle, followed by another swig of his drink, but I choose to stay silent until he speaks again.

'You can tell me what it is. In fact, I'm the best person to share a secret with because you know I'll have forgotten it soon enough,' he says, though he's not laughing now. 'If I can't remember how to operate the television or what I had for breakfast yesterday, I'm surely not going to remember anything you might tell me.'

'I don't have a secret,' I say again, but quieter and even less convincingly than the last time, and Joe clearly knows I am hiding something. But even I don't know what it is yet, so I couldn't tell him even if I wanted to. I need time to think about this, though even if I get it, I doubt I'd tell Joe what is going on in my head because I don't know him well enough. He might think that his declining memory means he is a perfect sounding board for any confessions, but could I really trust him? What would stop him telling Parker?

And what if my secret is so bad they have no choice but to tell the police?

I need to say something to Joe to get him to drop this and I think I have just the thing.

'You're not the only one with memory troubles,' I admit to him, and he turns away from the ocean and looks at me. 'I don't have dementia, but I do have something wrong with my brain.'

'You do?'

I nod and regret for a second the fact that I turned down a drink – I feel like I could use one now.

'Ask me what I did yesterday or last week and no problem, I can tell you, for the most part, anyway,' I explain to Joe. 'But ask me what I did a couple weeks ago, and it gets foggy. Ask me what I did last month, and I can't remember at all. Ask me what I did last year and, honestly, I don't even remember being alive.'

Joe looks puzzled by my explanation of my issues, but I'm being totally honest with him, which I think he realises, because he quickly looks sympathetic.

'You've got amnesia?' he guesses.

'I don't know. Maybe. Probably.'

'Do you know what caused it?' he asks, but I shake my head.

'No. I don't know a lot of things. I just know what I'm not supposed to do.'

'Which is?'

I almost say 'watch the news', but that'll give away too much, so I leave it and ask a question of my own.

'Are you going to tell your son?' I ask nervously. 'Maybe you should. I should have told him before he gave me this job. I doubt I'm the right person to be giving you care.'

Joe is quiet for a moment, and I have absolutely no idea what his response is going to be. But when it comes, it surprises me.

'I won't tell my son what you've told me,' he says. 'Like you, I'll probably forget it soon enough anyway. Like I said, you're not the only one with secrets, so whatever your secret is, it's safe with me. At least it is as long as you go and make me a sandwich.'

I laugh, Joe's jokey last line doing the trick of breaking the tension that had been building between us.

'Do you mean that? You won't tell anybody what I just told you?' I ask, seeking further reassurance.

'Hey, I said it, didn't I? Why would I lie?'

I don't know, but that doesn't mean it's not possible. But here's the problem. Either I trust Joe now or I don't, and if I don't, I might as well leave here and never come back.

I take a few seconds to make my decision before I get up, though I'm not headed for the door. I'm going into the kitchen to make lunch. I'm still troubled by my thoughts on the news report and how I might know the missing man in Chicago, but at least it seems I'm not in any immediate danger of being exposed.

Once it's made, I give Joe his meal and we spend the rest of my shift out on the balcony, him asking me a few things he already asked me yesterday, as well as repeating a few things, banal things, but things that show his memory is waning. But he doesn't ask me any more about my murky past, and when Parker arrives home, Joe gives me a quick wink to let me know not to worry about anything more being said, before asking me in a whisper not to mention the fact that he has an open whiskey bottle stashed away here.

'Were you trying to call me earlier?' Parker asks me as I'm getting ready to leave, and I realise I need an excuse for why I was ringing him.

'Oh, erm, don't worry about it. I was just going to check with you what Joe had for breakfast, but he told me.'

That white lie is good enough and, with that, I tell Parker

that I have to get going and I'll be back tomorrow. But I'm not sure if I will be, because between now and tomorrow, I am going to be spending as much time as I can trying to learn about that missing man on the news in case it stirs any more memories for me. I can use my phone to search, the one I bought when I got here that has no contacts in it other than Parker, my new employer. I also know there is an internet café near the beach just past my flat, so I could go and use a computer there if I want to.

By the time I make it home, I've been struck by the paranoid thought that someone might be able to see what I have been looking at online. Not wanting to have a suspicious browser history, I avoid the internet café and just enter my flat. I might still spend some time browsing the web on my phone, even if it is a bad idea, because there'll be no way I can sleep with all this in my head.

As I enter my bedroom, I think about the warning in my notebook and what Pippa might think if she knew I had ignored it. I feel bad for her, even if I don't really know her, at least not anymore, but what could I do? Joe wouldn't let me change the channel and now I can't rewind time.

I reach under my pillow for the notebook, as if reading it again will change something, which it won't, but I'll do it anyway, if only out of habit.

But there's a problem.

The notebook isn't here.

I pull the pillows off the bed then peel back the duvet, figuring it has to be here somewhere, but I still can't see it.

Maybe it fell down the back of the bed, so that's the next place I check, but still no luck.

Now I'm looking behind the bedside tables, opening drawers, rummaging through my wardrobe and eventually searching the rest of my flat, including the bathroom, even though I know my notebook never, ever leaves the bedroom.

It's no longer where it should be.

But I haven't taken it.

That means someone else must have.

TWELVE

PIPPA

Any hopes I have that the missing diary pages hidden beneath the floorboards in Darcy's old bedroom contain nothing incriminating are dashed when the person who's just read them asks me one very serious question.

'What the hell did Darcy do?' Dad wants to know, fear etched onto his face as he lowers the diary pages and looks up at me standing before him – out of breath and out of time to stop him from finding something terrible here.

It's not been long since I rushed into this house and tried to get my father's attention. Not long since I saw he had found the diary pages that had managed to elude me when I had searched this place three months ago. And not long, therefore, since Dad entered the world I have been forced to live in – the world where we realise that Darcy is not just some poor nurse who had a bad accident and lost her memory.

She is so much more than that.

'Give me those,' I say as I reach for the diary pages, but Dad swipes them away, though sadly not because he hasn't finished reading them. It's because he's not going to give them up until

I've explained what is written on the pages. Of course, it's tricky because I haven't read them myself. However, based on what I already know about Darcy's past, I can make a pretty good guess that whatever is written there is not good. There's also the fact these pages were hidden underneath the floorboards. Nobody hides anything in a place like that unless they don't want that thing to be found.

But Dad did find them.

'How?' I ask as I stare at the hole in the floor beside the bed where my sister used to sleep.

'I was kneeling under the bed, moving some boxes around when I felt a weak spot in the floor,' Dad tells me as he stares at the hole too. 'I pulled the rug back and realised one of the floorboards was loose. When I pulled it up, I saw something was hidden under there.'

I wish more than anything that I had been the one to notice that loose floorboard – then I'd have been the one reading the diary pages. But it didn't work out that way – where my sister is involved, things are rarely perfect.

'Tell me what you know,' Dad says as he takes a seat on the edge of the bed. 'Tell me everything.'

I can see that pretending to be clueless is futile, so I simply take a seat beside Dad and, when I do, I see there is something he is holding along with the diary pages.

It's a photo of Darcy smiling.

And Laurence is right beside her, smiling too.

'It's the missing man from the news,' Dad needlessly points out to me. 'Did Darcy have anything to do with him vanishing?'

'Don't make me tell you,' I say. 'Honestly, you don't have to know and it's better if you don't. I can protect you if you don't know.'

'Protect me? I'm your father. I should be the one protecting you!'

'This isn't about some bully at school, Dad! This is much bigger than that! You can't protect me from this because I know too much, and I've also done too much. But you can protect yourself. Stay oblivious to it. You and Mom, stay out of it. That way, even if everything goes wrong, you two won't get in trouble.'

That seemed perfectly reasonable as I said it, but Dad disagrees quickly.

'Me and your mother have a right to know what our children have been doing,' he snaps back. 'Especially if it relates to anything illegal and, from what I have read in this diary, it certainly sounds like it does!'

Dad thrusts the diary pages into my hands, allowing me to have a quick read of them so I know exactly what has got him so worked up. I had already figured it related to Laurence, but as I read the missing entries, I realise just how bad it is.

May 16th – I probably shouldn't be writing this. I might scribble it out when I've finished or maybe I'll burn it. That's because what is happening is dangerous. He suggested something yesterday and he repeated it again today. He has an idea about how we can be together sooner. He knows how we can get rid of his wife. He wants to kill her. And he wants me to do it.

I already knew the story of Darcy caring for Laurence's sick wife, Melissa, and then him embarking on an affair with Darcy. I also knew from the previous diary entries I had found, the ones not hidden under the floorboards, that Darcy was in love with Laurence and was frustrated that she couldn't spend more time with him, though it was understandable because his wife needed his attention too. There had been nothing to suggest that Darcy was rushing anything, but it is clear from the diary entries that Laurence was growing impatient, and wanted a way to speed up his wife's descent into death by helping her along the way.

He wanted Darcy to kill his wife and, foolishly, my sister, blinded by love or just confused by fear, was stupid enough to not only entertain the idea but write it down in her diary. She obviously knew it was a bad idea because she mentioned that she shouldn't be writing it and that she might burn it afterwards so nobody could read it.

But she didn't burn it.

She buried it.

Then she had her accident and forgot it was still here.

I sift through the pages of the diary as Dad sits silently beside me, unwilling or unable to say another word until I have finished reading. By the time I've done that, several stomach-churning sentences are stuck in my mind forever.

May 19th – Laurence keeps going on about it. He thinks it's a good idea. I told him we can't do it. It's too cruel, and it's illegal. I could lose my job. I could lose everything. Though it's hardly as bad as what Melissa would lose – her life.

May 23rd – Laurence says we can have a dream life together when she's gone. Instead of being apart so much or only seeing each other when I go to care for Melissa, we could do fun things. Go on date nights. Vacations. One day, we could get a place together. It all sounds so dreamy. But Melissa is still alive, so this is all still so wrong...

May 26th – Laurence is not happy. Melissa seems to be getting better. I told him it's only a brief respite in her treatment and her cancer is still there, but he says this is taking too long. He says he's exhausted and can't carry on like this anymore. He told me if she isn't gone soon, he's not sure we can carry on as we are.

May 27th – He gave me an ultimatum. Either Melissa goes or he goes. I can't lose him. I love him. What do I do?

There is only one more entry and it comes a few days later. It doesn't say much, but it says more than enough.

June 1st – I told Laurence we'll do it.

The pages in my hands have become stained by a couple of tears that have rolled down my cheeks and dropped onto the paper as I read the entries. I am upset not just because of the situation my sister had grappled with, but her ultimate decision. There are no more entries after that, but I recall from the media that Melissa's death was recorded as June fifth, so it came only a few days after this final entry. But I also recall something important, which is that Darcy changed her mind at the last minute and, despite preparing to inject Melissa with drugs that would kill her, she ultimately could not go through with it. That had been when Laurence had taken over and killed his wife himself. But Dad doesn't know that, so from his point of view, his daughter is a stone-cold killer. The same daughter he helped through nursing school, the one he was so proud of when she came up in conversation at dinner parties, the one he had a photo of in his home on graduation day.

He thinks she is disgraced. He might even think she is evil.

But he is wrong.

'She didn't do it,' I say firmly to my father as he holds his head in his hands. 'She didn't kill Laurence's wife. She got brainwashed by Laurence and almost got led astray, but she stopped at the last minute. *He* killed his wife, not Darcy. She is innocent. Of course she is, you know her as well as I do. You know she'd never do something like this. She was brainwashed by him. She was in love. She was lonely and none of us noticed it. It must have felt to her like Laurence was the only one who did, but we all wish he hadn't, because he used Darcy to get what he really wanted.'

I've said a lot in one statement, but I think the part that landed most with Dad is where I described Darcy as lonely. She had to have been to have fallen under the spell of such a rotten man like Laurence, to have an affair and contemplate murder and risk her entire personal and professional life for him. And what were her closest family members doing at the time? They were far too occupied with their own lives to notice.

'You knew about all of this, didn't you?' Dad retorts in disgust, and I have to nod.

'This is why you took Darcy away? This is why we can't know where she is? Because she's a criminal. She's on the run.'

'No,' I correct him. 'She's not a criminal, at least she hasn't done anything she didn't have to do.'

'What the hell does that mean?' Dad snaps back, his face a picture of disdain.

'It means she is still a good person. Laurence was the bad guy. Not Darcy.'

'Why are you talking about him in the past tense?' Dad asks, and I realise I'll have to explain that, but I've already resigned myself to giving him the full truth anyway by this point.

'Because he's dead,' I reply quietly as Dad's mouth hangs open in horror.

'Darcy had to do it. It was self-defence. He was going to kill her because her memory was returning, and she remembered what he had done to his wife!' I cry, defending my departed sibling because I'm the only one who can. 'Laurence had started seeing Eden, Darcy's colleague. That's why Darcy got into her accident. She found out that Laurence didn't really love her and when she sped away from his place, she crashed. Then, after the role-playing we did, she started having flashbacks, and she found Melissa's address and went there to see Laurence and get more answers. Eden was there too, and Laurence panicked that Darcy would remember it all and go to the police, so he tried to kill her. He made Eden steal some drugs from the hospital and planned to inject her, but Darcy got him first, then Eden ran away. I arrived on the scene shortly after. Then I told Darcy that she had to leave Chicago, just in case the police started looking.'

I've explained it all to Dad as openly and as honestly as I can, and I hope that will be it. But then Dad asks the pertinent question I should have known he was always going to ask.

'What happened to Laurence's body?'

'Please, don't make me tell you,' I beg my father, tears streaming down my face, but he tells me he has to know, so I ultimately confess to having dumped it in our city's famous lake, and if I thought Dad was shocked to hear what Darcy had done, he is just as stunned to hear about my behaviour.

Once our distressing conversation is over, Dad paces around the house, walking between piles of boxes while shaking his head and repeating over and over that he doesn't know what to do. I try telling him that all he has to do is stay quiet about this and it will be fine, while shamefully making sure to mention that, if he doesn't, both his daughters will go to prison and our family will be ruined forever. But in between our difficult conversation I'm also making sure to destroy Darcy's diary pages, doing to them what my sister should have done a long time ago and burning them, along with that photo she had kept of her and Laurence.

Stupidly, I think I've got the situation under control now.

I figure Dad just needs a little more time, that I can convince him to keep quiet and this will all settle down. But I'm wrong, though it's not Dad who is the problem.

It's my other parent.

Mom suddenly calls us and, when she finds out that we're together, she has something frightening to say that will make both our days go from bad to worse.

'I've got something to tell you,' she says, her voice shaking and her breathing heavy. 'And it's not good.'

THIRTEEN

DARCY

'Where are you?' I cry at the top of my voice, although asking a question of an inanimate object is hardly going to pay dividends.

My missing notebook can't answer me and tell me where it is, but I'm asking anyway because I've tried everything else. I've looked everywhere inside my apartment, but I cannot find it. I'm unable to shake the fear that somebody got in here while I was out and stole it from me.

I check my front door, but can't see any signs of forced entry, though it's hardly a secure barrier between the inside and out. Somebody could probably force this door open quite easily due to how thin and flimsy it is, or maybe they didn't even have to do that if they had a key to this place. Has the owner of this property been here? They shouldn't have without telling me, but they must have been; but they certainly shouldn't have touched any of my personal possessions.

Without any more luck finding what I need, I can't think of anything to do other than call the letting agency who handle my tenancy and demand to know why somebody has been in my apartment. The problem with that plan is there is no answer when I call the office, and I guess that's because the working day is over now. I'll have to wait until tomorrow, unless I want to send an angry message to my landlord, and I am about to do that when I hear a knock at the door.

I go to answer it, wondering if it could be my landlord coming back to apologise, telling me that he took the notebook by mistake while here on other business. But I open the door and see it's not him, it's my pervy neighbour. As well as giving off a strong scent of marijuana, his eyes linger on my body for several seconds too long before he makes eye contact with me.

'Heyyy,' he says in a very relaxed drawl, similar to how all the lazy surfer dudes around here used to speak to me when I was behind the counter at the café. 'Wanna hang out?'

'No, I don't,' I say to him, still unsure what his name is, and I go to close the door, but he sticks out a hand to stop me.

'Hey! What's wrong? We're friends, aren't we?' he says. 'And friends check up on each other.'

'I'm fine,' I say firmly before trying to close the door again, but his hand remains as an obstacle.

'Are you? I just heard you shouting out. Sounds like you need some help. Have you lost something?'

I stop trying to shut the door as a thought races through my mind.

Has he taken my notebook? He lives right next door to me. Maybe he saw me go out this morning and figured out a way to get in. We probably have the same type of key and, if the landlord is as useless as I suspect him of being, we might even have the same lock.

'Have you been in here while I was out?' I ask nervously.

'What? Me? No man, no way,' he replies, but is he telling the truth? I assume not, but he's hardly likely to admit to trespassing and theft, so there's no point asking him again. But maybe I can spook him into a confession.

'You're right. I have lost something and I'm just about to call the police to report it,' I say sternly. 'So if you know about anything that happened here today while I was out, now would be a good time to tell me about it.'

'I don't know anything,' he replies with a shrug, and the gormless expression on his face suggests he might be telling the truth. Then again, he looks like this most of the time, so it's hard to tell. Unfortunately, I don't want to call the police, not after what I saw on the news earlier and my fear that I could be connected to it, so I was just bluffing and it doesn't seem to have worked. But at least I am about to be left alone again.

'I guess I'll see you later, neighbour,' he says as he slowly takes his hand off my door and goes back to his own apartment. As I hear him go inside, I wonder if he has my notebook in there with him. Or maybe he's totally innocent. I have no idea. All I do know is that I need to find my notebook – it's important that I read it every day. Without it, I'll eventually forget everything written inside it.

Then I'll know absolutely nothing of my past.

Not wanting to risk that, I quickly find a piece of paper and a pen and write down everything I can recall from the notebook. Having only read it this morning before work, it's fairly fresh, so I can recount the names of the people inside it and their relationship to me.

Scarlett. Adrian. Pippa. Mom. Dad. Sister.

Next, I write down the two instructions Pippa had for me. *No news. Don't go home.*

Lastly, I go to write the home address. I know it was a place I was to only go to if there was ever an emergency, but this is where I stall.

I can remember the address was in Chicago and I think it was in a place called Winnetka. But that's about as much as I can remember. Damn it, I've forgotten the house number and street name. Whoever has my notebook has the information though, so I have to find them and therefore it, and with no other possible explanation as to why it's gone missing, I know I have to find the culprit fast.

Aware that I'm not going to get any more clues here, I head out, deciding to take a look around in the corridor outside my apartment, as well as the exterior of the building to see if there might be any clues there. I don't notice anything untoward in the corridor, no strangers lurking around, nor do I see anybody when I go outside the building. But now I'm out, I figure this is a good place to make my phone call to my landlord, and even if he doesn't answer, I can leave a very angry message on his voicemail either demanding to know why he has taken something of mine or how somebody else was able to gain access to my private property. Somebody like my creepy neighbour, who for all I know could be reading my notebook right now.

As expected, my landlord doesn't answer and, annoyingly, I discover he doesn't have a voicemail facility set up on his phone, so I can't leave the angry message I was planning on. That's lucky for him but unlucky for me, and I let out a cry of frustration that a few people walking back from the beach hear and frown at.

Too much is going on here. My notebook is gone and I saw a man on the news who I've been having nightmares about hurting. I need answers to some of it, or all of it, and I need them now, but I'm guessing the only people who can give them to me are my family. There's nothing else for it. I'll have to go to the internet café and search my family members' names and try and find them, and if I get a specific address, maybe I'll just leave Florida tonight and go there. I'll have to give up my job and my apartment, but that feels better than staying here where some stranger has my notebook and now knows as much about me as I do.

I turn and start walking to the internet café, and when I see it come into view, I quicken my pace before I can change my mind about this. But just before I get there, I see a couple of people I recognise walking towards me.

'Darcy? Hey, long time no see!'

Parker laughs at his joke as he comes to a stop with Joe alongside him, and it looks like the pair have been out for a walk ever since I left them. It's nice they've been doing that – I've certainly not been enjoying my time since then, but do I want Parker to know that as I stop and talk to him? Or will hearing about my problems only make everything worse?

'Is everything okay?' Parker asks me. 'You look a little flustered.'

'Yeah, fine,' I mumble, but he can seemingly read me like a book because he doesn't take that for a good enough answer.

'We're going to get some ice cream and it looks like you could use some. Come on, let's go,' Parker says, and while he has one arm interlinked with his father, he uses his spare one to link arms with me. It all happens very quickly, and despite Parker taking me off course, I can't deny it feels nice to be close to him. He clearly has no problem getting close to me either and, for a few seconds, it feels like all my problems and worries melt away, as this confident man leads me along the beach towards the nearest ice cream parlour. It almost feels like we could be a couple, or at least a couple and Joe, the man accompanying us, but that's OK, as there's a good reason that he shouldn't be left on his own. I guess I'm enjoying whatever this is because I forget about my need to track down my family or my notebook, and now all I'm thinking about is which ice cream flavour to get.

My problems seem less important when I'm in company, so maybe that's what I need to do.

Have company.

If my family could help me, they could be company, but they aren't here, so I guess they can't.

Little did I know it then, but at that moment, it was my family who could have done with *my* help...

FOURTEEN

PIPPA

I have no idea why Mom called Dad and told him that she needs us to go home urgently, but we're both in his car now on the way there and whatever it is, it must be bad because he tells me that Scarlett sounded very distressed.

'She was drinking when I spoke to her on the phone earlier,' I say to him as he steers us through the streets at sunset. 'Maybe she carried on. She could just be very drunk.'

'No, there's something wrong,' Dad replies, not taking into account my theory that alcohol might be causing her to be a little overdramatic. But I'm hoping I'm right. There's already been more than enough drama for one day.

As we drive on, I'm more than aware that the previous drama with the diary pages is still very much unresolved, which is why I broach the subject with my father now rather than leaving it to be discussed when my mother is present.

'What are you going to say to Mom?' I ask anxiously. 'Are you going to tell her about Darcy's diary and our connection to Laurence?'

'She's my wife, so I should tell her everything,' Dad begins, which doesn't sound good, but then he adds something. 'But she's your mother, and what her two children have done could break her heart or send her to an early grave, so in answer to your question, I don't know what I'm going to do.'

'Okay,' I say, nodding, because maybe this damage can be contained. 'If that's the case, best to stay quiet until we've had more time to think it through. If you really want to tell Mom in the future then I guess I can't stop you. But let's take it slowly and not rush into anything. We don't want to make a mistake.'

'Because we'll all end up in prison if we do?' Dad assumes, turning away from the road for a second to look at me. 'That's what you're getting at, isn't it? If we make a mistake then we go to prison. I guess you're right. We would all go. Darcy. You. And now me.'

'You? No, you wouldn't be in trouble,' I suggest, but Dad just scoffs at my naïvety.

'Of course I would. I've just heard you confess to disposing of a body, a body my other daughter was responsible for. Not to mention I've read evidence of another crime involving some poor woman who was murdered by the husband who was supposed to be helping care for her. If I don't take that information to the police, and I'm obviously not going to, then I am almost as guilty as everybody else in this now. A jury would certainly see it that way.'

Unfortunately, Dad is right. Any impartial third party would say he is incriminated now because he hasn't reported any of what he has discovered to the police, but of course, there's a very good reason for that. By doing so, he'd solve a puzzle that everyone in Chicago is desperate to solve, but at the same time, he'd destroy the most important thing to him.

Family.

'Stop talking about police and juries and evidence,' I suggest, trying to improve his mood, though it's not an easy task. 'You need to stay calm. I've managed it for these last three months and so has Darcy.'

'It's that easy, is it? Just stay quiet and carry on with life as normal?' Dad asks sarcastically.

'No, of course not. I didn't say that. Don't you think I've struggled with this? It's been hell, but what is the alternative? I made a decision in the moment to help my sister, my sister who had done nothing wrong, and I stand by that. I thought you'd understand.'

'Oh, I understand that part all right,' Dad says as we cruise past a green traffic signal, and we're getting close to the house now. 'What I don't understand is how I was able to raise two daughters capable of doing such crazy things and keeping it from their parents.'

'We were trying to protect you and Mom!'

'And has it worked?' Dad cries. 'Darcy left, and your mother has been a wreck ever since. Now I've discovered the truth and how do you think I feel? Now I'll forever worry that the police will take you and your sister away. What kind of life is this going to be for us all?'

'I'm sorry, but what do you want me to do? I'd do anything to make this better, but I can't. I was just trying to help Darcy!'

'So you keep saying! But she's not here helping you, is she? Nor is she here helping me or your mother. So where is she? What is she doing that is so much more important than being here with us while we try and deal with all of this?'

I can see Dad is up for an argument and is clearly ready to put a lot of the blame on Darcy, which isn't fair for two reasons: one, she isn't here to defend herself, and two, she isn't to blame for this at all. Laurence manipulated her, and even when she did the right thing and refused to kill Melissa for him, she still paid the price for his actions and, ultimately, had to kill him to save herself. She ended up hurt and is still unwell, so I will not have him put this on her.

'If Darcy was the villain in all this then I wouldn't have helped her,' is all I can say to Dad now. 'But she isn't, so I helped, and here we are. Now I need your help, Dad. I need you to protect our secret.'

Dad takes his eyes off the road to look at me again and, finally, I think he is going to relent and stop debating this issue, at least for a short while. Or maybe it's just the fact that we are almost at our destination now. Whatever it is, the pair of us are silent as he steers us onto Sherwood Crescent and I see my parents' huge house come into view up ahead.

I love this house, and I love this street, and I know I was incredibly fortunate to spend so many years living here before I moved out of the family home. Our first house, the one we have just come from, is nice, but this is something else. This is the kind of property that people dream about, save an entire lifetime for, and in some cases, kill for. But my parents obtained it through nothing but sheer hard work and I am very proud of them for that. Too bad they aren't exactly proud of me at the moment, but I'm hoping I can change that, and right here might be a great place to start.

If I can sort out whatever problem Mom has got, maybe that will go some way to redeeming me in her eyes for sending Darcy away, and possibly in Dad's eyes for having such terrible secrets. Or maybe I'm being a little too hopeful, but optimism has to trump pessimism every time, otherwise what's the point?

However, as Dad and I got out of his car and made our way to the front door, I was not to know then that I was severely underestimating the size of the problem that Mom had.

I was still blissfully unaware of the sheer nightmare that awaited us when we walked inside.

Dad is right about me. I am naïve at times, but in this case, so was he.

That's because neither of us could have foreseen what Mom was about to show us when we walked inside.

FIFTEEN

'What's going on?' I ask Mom when I see her nervously pacing around in the hallway as Dad and I enter.

'Are you okay?' Dad asks, sending another question Mom's way, but she doesn't answer, choosing to just keep walking rather than talking, which isn't very helpful, considering we've driven all the way over here to find out what is the matter.

'Mom! What is it?' I demand to know, and my raised voice gets her to stop pacing and look at us. But before she can speak, somebody else does.

Somebody we had no idea was here.

'Hey! Let me out of here! Open this door!'

I spin around and look in the direction of the female cries for help before realising they come from the study. I can see the study door is shut, but the cries definitely came from behind there, and now I can hear banging on that same door.

Is somebody locked in there?

'Who is that?' Dad asks, as horrified as I am.

'Help me! Let me out! You can't do this to me!' come more desperate cries, and while I don't recognise who the voice belongs to, it's not as if this would be any better if I did.

Why does it seem like Mom has somebody locked away in the study?

'Mom, start talking now,' I urge my mother, rushing to her and putting both my arms on her shoulders so she can't move or get away. I notice that she feels very weak once I have taken hold of her. I can smell alcohol on her breath, but she doesn't seem to possess any of the extra boldness or courage that she usually has when she's been drinking.

I've not seen her looking this vulnerable since Darcy had her accident and we were at the hospital, wondering if she was going to survive. That tells me, as if the trapped woman in the study wasn't enough, that this must be bad if it's got Mom so troubled again.

'Who is it? Who is in there?' I demand to know, shaking my mother's shoulders, and my desperation to get the answer is matched by the desperation of the woman to get out of that study as she keeps pounding on the door. It's hard enough to hear myself think with all this noise, but through all the commotion, Mom answers me, letting Dad and me know exactly what we are dealing with here.

'It's Eden,' Mom says quietly.

'Eden?' Dad repeats. I let go of Mom's shoulders and take a step back from her before glancing nervously at the study door again. So now I know who it is in there.

It's Darcy's ex-best friend and colleague.

The person who started dating Laurence while Darcy thought he was in love with her.

It's the person who stole the drugs from the hospital that Laurence planned to use to kill my sister.

Most recently, it's the woman who ran away, just after my sister killed Laurence, and hasn't been seen since.

'What is she doing here?' I ask, afraid of the answer – it can't be good.

'She's looking for Darcy. She says she needs Darcy to tell

the truth about what happened so the police won't arrest her when she resurfaces,' Mom replies as all three of us keep staring at the door, which is shaking every few seconds when Eden gives it another thump. 'What is she talking about? What truth does she mean?'

I look at Dad and he knows as well as I do what Eden is here for. She's here because, at the moment, the police are hunting for Laurence and Eden. They won't have much luck finding Laurence – or at least not a walking, talking version of him anyway – but they could find Eden. If they do, they will want to know what happened to him and, because she wouldn't have a very good answer, the chances are Eden would be arrested on suspicion of harming Laurence. Of course, she's actually innocent, at least in terms of Laurence and his body being at the bottom of Lake Michigan, but she'd probably have a hard time explaining that. But she would make sure to mention somebody who could help the investigation.

Darcy.

I always knew it was a worry having Eden out there somewhere in the world, possibly ready to pop back up at any time and ruin things. But after three months, I'd figured she'd found a way to lie low herself and start a new life elsewhere. I assumed she wouldn't come here or go to the police because that would risk her being arrested. She stole the drugs from the hospital that were found in Laurence's house, next to his blood. It wouldn't take a genius detective to come to the conclusion that she killed her boyfriend and ran away. But that detective would be wrong. My sister did the killing. Eden is guilty of theft and would lose her job. She is also guilty of assisting Laurence in imprisoning my sister while they prepared to kill her. However, she is not guilty of homicide.

But I cannot have her telling the police that.

'I'll speak to her,' I say as I step towards the door, but Dad shoots out an arm and stops me.

'What? What are you going to say?' he wants to know, as Mom looks puzzled.

'What is going on here?' she asks, figuring that Dad and I are obviously in the know on something that she isn't.

'Wait, how did you even get her locked in there?' I ask Mom, trying to fathom that part out, and now Mom's the one who looks like she doesn't want to answer a question.

'I had no choice. She kept talking about going to the police and something about Darcy and how this was all her fault. I didn't know what she meant, but it was obviously bad news for Darcy, so I panicked and...' Mom's voice trails off, but Dad urges her to finish her sentence.

'I hit her,' Mom confesses, and that was not what either of us expected to hear.

'You did what?' Dad cries.

'I had no choice! She was saying that Darcy had hurt that man on the news. Laurence, is it? I thought she must be lying, but she seemed so sure about it, and she kept insisting she would go to the police. I had to do something. I had to stop her leaving. So I used that.' Mom gestures to an umbrella lying at the bottom of the stairs.

'You hit her with an umbrella?' Dad says, visibly stunned that his wife was capable of such an act.

'What else could I have done? Let her go to the police and tell them Darcy had hurt someone? She hasn't, has she? Darcy is innocent, right?'

That's a very long conversation and one I don't have time for right now, not when there's a very live problem in this house, or more specifically, in the study.

'How badly did you hurt her?' I tentatively ask Mom.

'Enough to slow her down. She's bleeding from her head a little,' Mom admits.

Dad starts panicking, but I tell him to calm down – that won't help us.

'So what? You hit her and then pushed her into the study and locked the door?' I ask, trying to fill in the blanks, and Mom confirms that's what happened, more or less.

'Let me out!' Eden shouts again, her voice pained but the lock still holding firm. It's clear there's only one possible way she is getting out of there. That's if the door is opened from this side.

But is that a good idea?

'Okay, here's what's going to happen,' I say after taking a deep breath. 'Dad, you're going to take Mom into the kitchen and you're going to explain everything to her. Everything you found back at the other house and everything I've told you since. Okay?'

Dad doesn't exactly look thrilled at that assignment, but given what's happened here tonight, there's no way we can get away with not bringing Mom into the loop now, so I guess that settles the debate we were having in the car on the way over here. However, the question of how much Mom can be trusted given her drinking problem is one we'll have to answer at some point. But before we can properly ponder that, Dad has another question for me.

'What are you going to do?' he asks me, aware that I've not given myself a task yet.

'I'm going to go into the study and speak to Eden,' I reply, trying to make myself sound more confident about this than I am. 'And I want you to promise me something. Whatever happens, do not open the door unless I tell you to. Okay?'

'Pippa, what are you going to do?' Dad repeats, clearly needing more of an answer.

So I give him the clearest one I can.

'I need to do this for our family,' I say before swallowing hard and stepping towards the study door.

SIXTEEN

'I'm going to unlock this door!' I call into the study once I've built up the courage. 'I don't want to hurt you, Eden, so step back and let me enter, and then we can talk about letting you go.'

I wait to see how my words have landed, but as much as the prisoner in the study is going to have to trust me, I'm going to have to trust her too. For all I know, she might be holding a weapon of her own, one similar to Mom's umbrella, and she might be planning on hitting me with it as soon as I walk in. I'll have to be on my guard, and I'll take the umbrella with me just in case it needs using again. But there's no way of resolving this situation unless I can talk to Eden face to face, so I'm going to have to open this door at some point.

That point is now.

I look back over my shoulder to make sure that Mom and Dad are out of the way and in the kitchen like they should be, and they are, and then I turn the key that Mom used earlier to start this whole ordeal.

The door unlocks and I brace myself for Eden to try and force herself out of the room, but that doesn't happen and, as the door opens, I spot her standing beside my father's desk, a safe enough distance away from me. She looks anxious, dishevelled, afraid – basically like a woman who has been in hiding but has reached breaking point and needs respite now.

As it turns out, I was right about one thing.

She is holding something that could hurt me.

'Put the lamp down,' I say calmly. 'I'm not here to hurt you.'

'Then let me go,' Eden snaps back. 'Your mother is crazy. She hit me over the head! Look!'

Eden gestures to the blood on her forehead, just below her hairline, the wound from Mom's umbrella visible and surely very sore. But Mom wouldn't have done such a thing if she didn't think it was necessary, and once Dad has finished explaining things to her in the kitchen, she will realise just how necessary it actually was.

'I'm sorry about that,' I say as I cautiously enter the room, then slowly close the door behind me, though I make sure not to turn my back on Eden in case she rushes at me. Once it's closed and it really is just the two of us, I know what happens next is all on me, rather than Mom and Dad, who are under strict instructions not to interfere with what goes on in here.

'Why are you closing the door? I thought you were letting me go?' Eden says, and she raises the lamp a little as if she's figuring out whether she's going to have to use it at some point because I'm lying to her.

'We just need to have a private conversation and I don't want anybody else to hear it,' I say softly. 'Take a seat.'

'No,' Eden replies, not interested in sitting down behind Dad's desk, even if his large leather chair looks comfortable. But I can't blame her. I wouldn't sit down either if I was in her position. She must be so afraid. But she's not the only one. At least I have the upper hand here because I'm on home soil, though that will only help me if I make it count.

'Why did you come here?' I ask. 'Why couldn't you just stay

wherever you were and stay away from us? You didn't need to turn up here.'

'Yes, I did! What other choice have I got? I didn't cause Laurence to go missing! I don't know where he is! The last I knew, when I ran from his house, he was alive and well. But now he's gone and his face and mine are all over the news. The police are looking for me and if they find me they'll think I hurt him! But I've done nothing wrong!'

'Nothing?' I snap back when Eden's rant ends. 'So you didn't steal drugs from your workplace and plan to use them with Laurence to kill my sister?'

That shuts her up, but only for a second.

'Yes, but I didn't hurt her. I helped her! I stopped Laurence and we were both running for the door. I got away. I thought Darcy did too.'

'She didn't,' I say with a sad shake of my head. 'Laurence caught her.'

'Oh my god,' Eden cries. 'What happened then?'

My hesitation in answering says it all.

'She killed him?' Eden asks, fear in her eyes.

'It was purely self-defence!'

'Then why didn't she call the police? She could have resolved all of this! She wouldn't have got in trouble for it, the police wouldn't be looking for him and everyone in Chicago wouldn't think that I was the one who hurt him!'

'She thought it was too risky to call the cops and I agreed with her,' I explain. 'They might not have believed her, especially not with her history. The memory loss, the confusion – any detective could have spun a story about her being unreliable, and therefore dangerous. And then there was the issue of the stolen drugs from the hospital, the ones you took. They would've needed to be explained and how would Darcy have done that? To the police, it would have looked like those drugs were purposely stolen so they could be used in a crime, and they were, except it was you who took them and you and Laurence who were going to commit that crime. How was it fair that my sister was left to answer for that?'

'How is it fair that people think I had something to do with Laurence going missing?' Eden retorts. 'I'm innocent. I haven't killed anybody! I've been living in cheap motels on the edge of the city, hiding away all day and burning through what little savings I have just to survive. But now my cash has run out and I'm screwed. But I can't go back to my normal life unless Darcy explains all this to the police, so that's why I'm here. I need your sister to help me like I helped save her life. So where is she?'

'She's not here,' I say, making sure to maintain strong eye contact with Eden so she can hopefully see that I am being honest. 'She's a long way from Chicago and she's never coming back. So she can't help you. You can only help yourself now. You need to leave Chicago too. Start a new life. Don't let anybody know who you really are, and they won't find out. You can do it. It's your only option.'

'No, it's not,' Eden says, shaking her head as tears well up in her eyes. 'There is another option. I go to the police and tell them what you just told me. Sure, I'll get in trouble for stealing from the hospital and hiding for so long, but so what? At least I won't be blamed for anything worse, and I'll only lose my job, not my freedom. At least I'll be able to carry on with my life, or whatever's left of it, without having to be looking over my shoulder forever! I'll be able to return to my home, get another job, have some semblance of an existence, which is a lot more than I have right now.'

Eden is extremely distressed, as she might well be given her circumstances, and this is not going well. This situation is threatening to get out of control, and I need to keep it contained. But how?

'We could give you some money,' I suggest. 'My parents have plenty of it. You said you're out of cash and that's why you're here, but we could help you. We could get you set up somewhere else. You wouldn't need to go to the police then. This could be the fresh start you need.'

I haven't discussed that option with my parents, but if it's the only way to keep Darcy safe, I'm sure they'll go for it. And they do have lots of money, which I'm sure Eden has already noticed as she stands in this decadent house.

'I don't want a fresh start! My life is here!' Eden cries, not saying what I was hoping she would. 'And what about Laurence?'

'What about him?'

'People need to know what happened to him. Where is he?'

That is not information I would divulge to anybody other than my closest family members, and even then, it was only because I had to, so I ignore that question and try again.

'You're getting confused here,' I say, taking a step towards Eden. 'You're acting like you have control, but you don't. You have one choice. You take the offer I'm giving you and start afresh elsewhere, never to breathe a word of this to anyone again. Or else.'

'Or else what?'

I don't really want to have to say it, so I wait until Eden figures it out.

'You'll hurt me?' she cries when it registers. 'Is that it? You're threatening me?'

'All I'm saying is that I will do whatever it takes to protect my sister,' I explain. 'Just like my parents will do whatever it takes to protect their daughter. So if it's a choice between you or Darcy, we pick Darcy every time.'

Eden lowers the lamp now, though it doesn't look like a conscious decision, more a sign that she realises she has no choice but to comply or she's never getting out of this room alive. It's several minutes after I first invited her to take a seat that she sits down at Dad's desk, letting go of the lamp entirely before putting her head in her hands.

I give her the time she needs to come to terms with this, glancing through the window that looks out on the front of the house to make sure there aren't any more uninvited guests on their way here this evening. But the street is quiet, as it nearly always is, and it will stay quiet as long as Eden doesn't do anything stupid.

'Fine,' she says after a nerve-wracking minute. 'I'll take your money and I'll stay quiet.'

'You'll leave Chicago for good and never come back?' I ask, needing confirmation.

Eden nods.

'Yes. I'll go tonight,' she replies.

It seems I've gotten my way and that's good news, but I have a few more questions.

'Where will you go?' I ask.

'I don't know.'

'I'd like to get the sense that you have some kind of plan.'

'California, maybe.'

'Do you know anybody there?'

'No, isn't that the point?'

'I'm just making sure,' I say. 'What about family and friends here? You won't ever be tempted to get in touch with them?'

'No. I don't have much family and I can make new friends.'

Eden seems like she is on board with this, so I guess it's time to invite my parents into the conversation so we can go through the details a little more.

'The door is unlocked,' I say. 'Why don't you go and get yourself cleaned up?'

Eden looks at the door and doesn't waste any time getting up and going towards it. I watch her as she goes, but just before she can leave the study, I have a question for her.

'You didn't ask me how much,' I say quietly.

'What?' she says, pausing by the door.

'You haven't asked me how much money we are going to give you,' I reply. 'If I was you, I would have wanted to know the exact amount I was going to get if I was having to start a new life. It seems quite an important detail.'

Eden stares at me for a second and, as I study her face, I'm desperately looking for any sign that the doubts I'm feeling are unwarranted. But I don't find any reassurance in her expression and, a moment later, all doubt is removed when Eden pulls the study door open and runs out into the hallway.

I knew it. She was just bluffing. She had no intention of taking our money and starting afresh. She was just saying what she had to for me to let her out of this room alive.

And now she's out.

I run out of the study and see Eden reaching for the handle on the front door. Just before she can pull it open, I grab her by the hair and drag her backwards, reminding myself that this is the woman who almost allowed Laurence to kill my sister. Without Eden's part in this, Laurence probably wouldn't have ended up dead and Darcy wouldn't have been forced to leave the city. Eden is not an innocent woman – that's what I tell myself as I drag her back into the study, ignoring Mom and Dad's questions as they call out from the kitchen to find out what is going on. I ignore them and I ignore Eden's cries for help. Most of all I ignore the voice in my head that tells me this might be a bad idea, as I pick up the lamp and raise it above my head.

I ignore everything as I hit Eden over the head with that lamp until she stops moving.

Only when I stop hitting her and look down at the body on the carpet do I realise that I'm even more like my sibling than I realised.

We are sisters.

We are nurses.
And now we are both killers.

SEVENTEEN

DARCY

'Are you okay?'

I look to Parker sitting beside me on the sand and he obviously just noticed that I shivered. But it wasn't the cooling temperature that caused it now that the sun has gone down in Florida. It was weird, but it felt more like a warning chill, or a sense that something is wrong somewhere. I don't know what it could be relating to. Needing an answer for Parker, I just blame it on the cooler evening air.

'I'm just a bit cold,' I say, rubbing my hands over my arms to warm them up and reinforce my white lie, and Parker buys it.

'Maybe we should get going,' he suggests, and that's not a bad idea – we have been here for a while. We've been sitting on the sand, surrounded by other people who are enjoying an early evening outdoors, ever since he and his father bumped into me while I was out walking earlier. My head was spinning as I worried about my missing notebook and who might have taken it, and at first I thought encountering the pair was more of a hinderance than a help. But that was before Parker invited me for ice cream and, ever since he did, I've begun to feel a little better about things.

I still don't know where my notebook is and I'm still worried about it, but tonight has given me something I've not had in a very long time.

Genuine company.

The three of us had made our selection of ice cream, Parker choosing chocolate, Joe opting for vanilla while I went for toffee, and after Parker kindly paid for it all, we came to the beach and sat down to enjoy it. But we didn't all sit together, as Joe preferred to sit on the stone wall a few yards away, while we sat on the sand, though only because, as Parker put it, Joe likes his own company from time to time. But that was okay, as it gave me and Parker the chance to talk a little more privately than if Joe had been with us, and therefore the conversation was a better one for it.

'I'm happy to stay for another five minutes if you and your father are,' I say in answer to Parker's suggestion that we get going, and when Parker agrees, I guess he's happy to stay too. I'm glad about that because if he leaves I'll be alone again, alone with my worries and problems, and that feels far worse than being here with a man I am warming to the more I spend time with him.

'Great,' Parker says before glancing at his dad to make sure he's okay, but he is. He looks perfectly happy sitting and watching a few skateboarders rolling past along the beachfront. Joe has seemed very content to be out here this evening, watching the world go by, and I suppose it's a welcome break for him from his apartment, which must feel increasingly like a prison, given how much more time he spends there as opposed to when he was in full health.

'He's looking well,' I say to Parker with a smile. 'Considering what's going on beneath the surface, anyway.'

'Couldn't the same be said about everyone?' Parker replies, not quite following the more positive note I was trying to stick to, but actually saying something incredibly honest and revealing in such a short response.

He's right, of course. Most of us look fine on the outside. But it's often a different story within.

He's certainly right about me.

However, it's not me I want to talk about now, nor am I the one with problems that I think Parker is hinting at. It sounds like he has a few of his own and, as we're here and he's been so nice to me so far this evening, I feel it would be rude of me not to ask him if he's okay.

'It's my girlfriend,' he says after I've enquired. 'Things aren't exactly great with her.'

'Do you want to tell me about it?' I offer, realising this is the first time he has mentioned to me that he is in a relationship. I already knew about his girlfriend, because Joe told me, but now Parker is willingly divulging that information himself.

'We're not getting along anymore,' he replies, proving that he is comfortable to open up about this to me, which gives me a warm feeling, even if it's a difficult topic to discuss.

'I'm sorry to hear that. Is this a recent thing?'

'No, it's been like this for a while. Gradually got worse. Now it's really bad.'

'How bad?'

My latest question is very probing, and I worry I've pried too much, but Parker doesn't seem fussed.

'I won't bore you with the details, but let's just say something has happened that we can't come back from.'

I instantly wonder if he is referring to an affair or something where trust has been broken between the pair, but I won't press him on that. It could be too much.

'I'm sorry,' is all I can think to say again, though I'm wondering if it was his actions that led to this relationship breakdown or the actions of his partner.

'What's her name?' I ask tentatively.

'Irene.'

'How long have you guys been together?'

'Four years.'

That's longer than I thought it would be. Parker's relationship is obviously more serious than some brief fling. Do I feel a little jealous of this Irene? Not exactly, if things are clearly going bad between her and Parker, though I presume the years leading up to this point were fun, at least in the beginning, anyway. Maybe that's what I'm jealous of. The fun of a new relationship. The spark. The lust. And the love that eventually blossoms. Not having any of that in my life is just one of several reasons why I feel so unhappy at present.

'Can't you talk things through?' I wonder.

'I think it's too far gone for that.'

'It can't be that bad, can it?' I ask, pressing for more details.

'I think we're over,' Parker tells me now, sounding very sure of that. 'It's time to try something else.'

I don't know if he means for that 'something else' to be me, but I can't help but look at Parker after he has just said it and, as I do, I see him turn to look at me – we hold each other's gaze for a couple of seconds too long.

If I wasn't so self-aware and self-conscious, I'd say it would actually be the perfect moment for one of us to go in for a kiss, but a kiss doesn't materialise, and that's probably for the best. Not only is Parker technically my boss, but the person he is paying me to care for is sitting nearby and could see us being very unprofessional if he was to look over.

I glance at Joe to see if he is watching us, at the part of the wall he has been sitting at all this time, yet when I do, I can't spot him.

'Where's your dad?' I ask, sitting up a little straighter on the sand as I look around for him, and Parker clearly had no idea he had moved either because he looks just as surprised as I am.

'Oh no,' Parker says, scrambling to his feet and sending a

little bit of sand onto my clothes, though I can't be annoyed because he's clearly worried where his dad has gone, and now I'm worried too.

'Dad!' Parker cries out, rushing to the wall where his father was sitting, before looking around through the moving mass of pedestrians, skateboarders and those sitting on the sand trying to enjoy a quiet evening. But they're all being disrupted now because Parker continues to call out to his father. But there is no response.

Realising I need to join the search, I get to my feet and start calling out for Joe while simultaneously scanning the beach for any sign of the man I've been looking after all day. But there are a lot of people here, the light is fading and, without knowing which direction he might have gone, it's no easy task to locate him.

'Dad!' Parker keeps calling, and he's decided to go left down the beachfront, which makes me decide to go right so we've got both directions covered.

I keep my eyes peeled for Joe while dodging a guy on his skateboard and a couple taking a selfie, but I'm still not having any luck. What if Joe has wandered off and got lost? What if he's confused and can't find his way back to us? What if he can't even remember who he is and where he needs to be?

I don't know if this has happened before, but I vow to ask Parker about it if we do find his dad, mainly so I can be wary of it in future while I'm caring for him. But I can't care for him again unless we find him, so I keep running and, as Parker and I continue to widen our search area, we're still not being reunited with the man we need to find.

And then I see him.

He's down on the beach, standing on the sand, right on the water's edge. It looks like he's just staring out to sea but he's not in the water, at least not yet, anyway. Now I've spotted him, I race towards him to make sure I reach him before he can enter the ocean.

'Joe!' I call out, and he turns to see me running at him, concern all over my face but relief flooding through me as I realise he is okay and Parker isn't going to have to be given any bad news about his father.

'Are you okay? We've been looking for you,' I say, out of breath. 'You wandered off.'

Joe keeps staring at me but doesn't speak, and I wonder if he even knows who I am and why I had to find him. But then he opens his mouth, though what he has to say is extremely disconcerting for a different reason.

'He needs to let her go,' Joe tells me, looking me square in the eyes.

'Sorry? What?' I reply, still catching my breath.

'Irene,' Joe adds, still looking serious.

'Parker's girlfriend?' I ask, and Joe nods.

'She's in danger,' he tells me. 'And now so are you.'

EIGHTEEN

PIPPA

It's not always easy to tell your parents things. It can be difficult to tell them about a new relationship with someone they don't approve of, or a drastic career change, or anything else that might give them cause for concern if they're worried you might be making a mistake. But in comparison to what I have to tell them now, the tricky conversations I've had to have with them in the past now seem ridiculously easy. Like the time I was considering dropping out of nursing school because I was finding it too hard, or the numerous nights I phoned home asking for money after I had frittered all mine while travelling.

I wish I was talking to them about simple things like that now.

Instead, I'm having to tell them that we need to get rid of a dead body.

'What's going on?' Dad asks me after he comes running out of the kitchen, ignoring my advice for him to stay where he is.

Mom is quickly behind him and looks just as worried as he does, although I'm about to make everything a whole lot worse for them. Right now, they can't see what is lying behind me on the carpet in the study. All they can see is me standing in the doorway to that room, blocking their view, and while I must appear flustered, they don't know why.

But they will in a second.

'I didn't mean to do it, but I had no choice,' I begin my defence, and I'm hoping it's a defence that only my parents will have to hear, and not a judge and jury at some point in the future.

'Do what?' Mom asks, while Dad looks around the hallway and, I imagine, looks for Eden, though he still can't see her yet.

'I tried to make a deal with her, but I could tell she wasn't going to stick to it, and then she tried to run,' I go on. 'I had to stop her. I had no choice. I had to do it. For Darcy and for all of us.'

'Pippa, what have you done?' Mom asks again, a mixture of fear and impatience in her voice. But I can't bring myself to say it, nor do I have to. Dad approaches me and, feeling far too weak to block him, I stand aside and allow him a full view into the study behind me.

'Oh my god,' he says when he sees Eden lying on the ground with blood pouring from her head. 'What the hell happened?'

'I hit her,' I say quietly, feeling far meeker than I did a few moments ago when I was wielding that lamp and turning it into a deadly weapon, all in the name of protecting myself and my family.

Dad rushes into the room to check her while Mom nervously approaches, leaving me to stand by, feeling helpless.

Why did Eden have to try and run? Why couldn't she have just done as I said? Why did this have to go so badly wrong?

In the blink of an eye, I've gone from somebody who aided a killer by disposing of a dead body and helping them get away, to a killer myself, and while that first crime was bad enough, this one feels very different.

This one feels far worse.

However, at this moment in time, only I know for sure that Eden is dead, which is why Dad is checking on her while Mom has a very serious question to ask.

'Is she alive?' she wants to know as we both watch Dad kneeling beside the body and feeling for a pulse. When he fails to find one, the look he gives the pair of us answers Mom's question immediately.

'What have you done?' Mom gasps, her face twisted in horror and her body seizing with fear, as if she is nervous just to be standing beside me, like I'm suddenly a danger to her as well. I'm not, of course, but I can see how bad this makes me look. In the blink of an eye, I've gone from being her precious, caring daughter to a callous killer – that must be a hell of a lot for any mother to process, especially one who only just found out that her other daughter has taken a life too.

'I had to do it!' I insist again. 'She was going to go to the police.'

'You killed her,' Mom retorts, still aghast.

'You locked her in here in the first place!' I cry with tears in my eyes, trying to make out like she started this, though of course, there's a huge difference between locking somebody in a room and beating them over the head with a blunt object until they stop breathing. But I'm still overcome with adrenaline, and I can't think straight, let alone properly talk about what I've just done.

'To reason with her, not kill her!' Mom cries, while I watch Dad check Eden one more time before grimly accepting his initial diagnosis that she's deceased.

'We need to deal with this, and we need to do it fast,' I say, more to him than to Mom, because he still seems quite calm whereas my mother is quickly losing her mind.

'I don't know what to do,' Dad admits as he sits back against the wall, slumped in the corner beside the body and, for a second, he looks like the frightened child I should be rather than the controlled parent I need him to be.

'Lake Michigan,' I say simply, two words that I know he will understand based on what I've already told him tonight.

That's where I put Laurence's body after Darcy killed him.

So that's where we need to put Eden's body too.

'I need time to process this,' Dad says, but I shake my head.

'No, there is no time. The longer we leave this, the more chance there is that we get caught. Oh my god, if I get caught, you know what I'll lose. I'll never see Campbell. He needs his mother, just like I need mine, so that's why we need to move Eden now. While it's dark outside, and before anybody can come here. We need to get rid of her and we need to clean up. Mom, you can do the cleaning in the study while me and Dad take the body to the lake.'

It sounds like a simple plan, and one that could actually work if everybody does as they are told, but it's a serious one and a shocking one – both Mom and Dad are just staring at me like I've suddenly grown an extra couple of heads.

'Just listen to yourself!' Mom exclaims. 'Who are you?'

'I'm sorry! I know it's a difficult thing to hear me talk about, but we don't have any time to waste. If we want to keep ourselves and Darcy safe then we need to be quick about this. If we hide Eden's body then nobody knows where she and Laurence are, and if that's the case, nobody ever has to know what Darcy did, or what we did. Then that'll be the end of it. All we'll have to do then is take our secret to the grave.'

I've laid out the facts as simply as I can, given the circum-stances, and thankfully one of my parents sees sense, snapping out of their terrified trance. It's Dad who slowly gets to his feet. But Mom is still standing beside me, fixed to the spot, and looking like she's going to need a lot more convincing before she makes a move in any direction.

'She's right,' Dad says, nodding at me. 'We have to act quickly, and we have to do this to protect Darcy.'

He looks at Mom and she eventually moves, though not in a positive way.

'I'm going to be sick,' she says as she puts a hand over her mouth before running into the downstairs bathroom and, seconds later, I hear retching coming from within.

Dad and I share a concerned look, the unspoken words between us being that, while we might be holding it together at present, there is someone who is not. Unless we can fix that issue, we aren't going to be safe. Suddenly, I have an idea how to make Mom feel at least a little bit better about what has happened here.

Heading for the bathroom and the continuing sounds of dry heaving, I take a deep breath, praying that what I'm about to say will work and do the important job of making Mom calm down. When I get there, I see her leaning over the toilet, her hands on the basin behind and her hair hanging down beside her face as she sucks in air before making a few most unsavoury sounds that tell me she is still feeling very nauseous.

'Mom, there is some good news here,' I say, which sounds totally outrageous given the circumstances, but it is true.

Perhaps it's the shock of what I've just said but Mom does turn around and look at me, with beads of sweat on her forehead and still gasping for oxygen, and she allows me to have my say.

'The reason I sent Darcy away was because we didn't know where Eden was and whether or not she was going to go to the police and mention Laurence,' I remind her.

Mom doesn't say anything, only wiping her forehead and still looking incredibly pale, so I have to fill in the blanks for her.

'Well, now that Eden is no longer a concern, it means Darcy doesn't have to hide away anywhere,' I say with a hint of a smile, but only a hint, because it seems very disrespectful to properly smile when a woman has lost her life here tonight.

My words land with Mom, and when they do I see a little colour returning to her face.

She's understood my point.

There is some good news here after all.

Maybe my sister can come home, and we can be a proper family again. Maybe we can put all this behind us.

Maybe.

NINETEEN

DARCY

'What do you mean?' I try to get Joe to tell me before Parker finds us. 'What do you mean Irene is in danger and so am I?'

Joe looks worried, but not because I've asked him to explain himself. It's because somebody is approaching behind me, and when I turn around I see Parker running across the sand towards us.

'Tell me,' I urge Joe during our last few seconds together, but he says nothing, and then Parker reaches us, surely spoiling any chance I have of getting his father to divulge further details about what he was referring to.

'Dad! What have I told you about wandering off?' Parker cries, looking concerned – or is it annoyed? It's hard to tell, especially with Joe's recent words still rattling around in my head, and while I was feeling very close to Parker only a few minutes ago, I'm now wary of him again.

'We were so worried,' Parker goes on, taking his father's arm. 'Come on. It's time to get you home.'

Joe goes along with his son's wishes, and as Parker marches his father across the sand and back to the beachfront, I'm left wondering what to do next. I decide to go after them. As I catch up, I'm debating whether or not to bring up what Joe just said to me. But I don't want to put the poor man on the spot, nor get him in trouble, so it might be best to do it when he's not around.

'Parker. Can I talk to you for a minute?' I ask, but no sooner have I done that than Joe shakes his head at me.

He clearly wants me to shut up, so I do, even after Parker asks me what's wrong.

'Nothing,' I reply, taking Joe's suggestion to stay quiet.

'Sorry about this. I really need to get my father home. We'll see you tomorrow, okay?' Parker says, ready to leave, but just before he can go—

'Wait,' I call out, and he stops, his hand still on Joe's arm.

'What is it?' he asks me, looking slightly irritated, but it's not just his evening that has not gone to plan.

'Erm, I'm not sure I'll be at work tomorrow,' I say nervously.

'Why not?'

'I've got a few things to sort out,' I say, which is an understatement. I still have the mystery of my missing notebook to solve, amongst many other things, one of which is figuring out if Parker is somebody I can really trust.

'But I need you,' Parker says, seeming genuine. 'You know I do. I need you to help me with my father. This is a full-time job – I made that clear.'

I look at Joe and he looks a little defenceless, standing beside his son, being held on to as if he is a disobedient child who will run away again if given the opportunity. But Parker takes a chance and lets go of his father, stepping towards me for a quiet word.

'I can pay you more if it's money you're worried about,' Parker says under his breath. 'I appreciate this might have been a bit distressing for you, having to go chasing my dad around a busy beach, and you might be worried about it happening when I'm not around. So how about I give you some more money?'

I'm still unsure, for several reasons, so Parker fills the silence.

'How about an extra fifty dollars a day?' he suggests.

'No, it's okay,' I say, feeling bad, but he shakes his head.

'That's still far cheaper than any nursing home I could put him in,' Parker goes on. 'Although maybe I'm running out of time on that front, if Dad is going to keep wandering off.'

'Has he done this before?' I ask, and Parker nods.

'Occasionally. Gives me quite the fright until I find him again. But it was you who found him this time. Thank you for that. Things could have been much worse if you hadn't helped me. He could have fallen into the water.'

This is the dilemma I face, I realise as I look at Parker, who seems truly grateful to me as well as nothing but worried for his father's health. He seems like a great guy, so why is it that his father keeps warning me about him? If Parker was that bad, surely Joe would have told somebody else about it by now and he wouldn't be left with him?

I know I'm unlikely to find out what is really going on if I just stop working for Parker, nor should I do that because it's imperative I know the truth. Either Joe is wrong and just saying things that he doesn't mean, in which case Parker really does need my help as much as he says he does. Or Joe is right, but, if that's the case, he is in danger and I should help him, rather than his son. I also need money and Parker has just offered me more of it. Without my notebook, I don't have much else to cling to that could improve my fortunes.

'Okay, I'll see you tomorrow,' I say quietly to Parker, who smiles and thanks me again, before returning to his father and leading him away in the direction of the older man's apartment.

As I watch them go, I think about what to do next. Should I go to an internet café and try and find out more about the names I recall from my diary, and where they might be specifically in

Chicago? Or should I go home and get some rest as it's getting late?

As I've already committed to working tomorrow, and finding out as much as I can about what is going on with the father and son duo, I opt to return to my own apartment. That'll also give me the chance to see if anything else has gone missing when I get back.

But it hasn't. Everything else is as I left it before I went for a walk and bumped into Parker and Joe. Now I'm tired and I need some sleep. When it comes, I dream of myself running around on the sand again like I was earlier in the night.

Only this time, I'm not running towards Joe.

I'm running away from his son.

TWENTY

PIPPA

The water on the lake is calm and quiet, in direct contrast to my heartbeat as it thunders away in my chest, the blood pumping around my body so fast and hard that I can barely hear myself think. I'd give anything to be as still and serene as the large body of water in front of me, but I never will be.

If I thought I was struggling before tonight, I'm really going to suffer once it's over with.

But it's not over yet – the dead body in the back of my father's car has not been deposited into the lake, so Dad and I could be caught if a witness was to wander by this part of the shoreline and catch us in the act.

'We need to hurry,' I say, stating the obvious, but needing to utter something that might get Dad moving. He hasn't budged since we parked up here a few minutes ago.

I directed my father to this part of the lake, having been here before. I know it's quiet here at this time of night, and I also know something just as important as that.

This is a place where dead bodies don't seem to get discovered.

It was three months ago when I pushed Laurence's corpse

into this part of the lake and watched it sink below the surface, the rocks I'd put into the dead man's pockets helping take him down to the depths where only the fishes who reside here would see his face. Trout, salmon and other marine life may have been unsettled initially when the body of a human began to sink down amongst them, but they have surely grown used to its presence now, wherever it lies on this lake bed, disintegrating over time until it's nothing but a pile of bones and a fully-fledged part of the ecosystem here, if it isn't already.

Safe in the knowledge that the body has not been disturbed yet, at least by anything other than aquatic life, I figure this is a good place to put another body.

It's time for Eden to reach her final resting place.

Or at least what I hope will be her final resting place.

Dad is quiet as we get out of the car and walk to the trunk. He lifts the lid and we both look down at the lifeless face of the woman I murdered two hours ago. In that time, we have moved her body from the study to Dad's car, which was conveniently parked inside the garage rather than on the driveway in full view of all the neighbours. Then we drove it here while Mom stayed at home, hopefully doing as I told her to and scrubbing the floor of that study to remove any blood, as well as smashing the lamp into as many tiny pieces as she can and disposing of it safely. But I'll have to trust that Mom is keeping her end of the bargain, just like she has to trust that we are keeping our end. To do that, Dad and I now need to work as a team to get the corpse into the water.

'I'll take the upper half,' I say, not because I want to be closer to Eden's broken skull but because it's easier on Dad if he takes the lower half, holding onto her legs rather than the end where the blood is.

I put my hands under Eden's shoulders and lift, and I can feel the bones in her back as I hold onto her. She's a burden to carry, but less so with my father's help, so it's the burden on my soul that is the hardest part about all of this.

We carry Eden the short way to the water's edge before we start to swing the body slightly, building up enough momentum to propel the corpse as far into the lake as possible, rather than allowing it to fall too close to shore and risk landing on shallower ground.

'One, two, THREE!' I cry, and on my last count we each let go of our section of the body. We watch as Eden flies through the air for a second before she crashes into the water, disrupting the still surface and sending small waves out in all directions.

As I watch the ripples fanning out around her, Eden sinks down quickly thanks to the rocks in her pockets, her face the very last thing I see before she vanishes and, seconds later, it's as if nothing has entered the water at all.

The splashing sound she just made is quickly replaced by a silence that is comforting and disturbing in equal measure. It's comforting because if everything is quiet then it probably means nobody else is here and saw what we did. If they were, they'd surely be gasping, or screaming, or at least running to get away from the two criminals they have watched in action. But on the other hand, it's disturbing – there's nothing to distract either of us from what we've just done, nor is there anything either one of us could say to make the other feel better.

At least I had something to say to make Mom feel better earlier. As I had hoped, telling her that Eden's demise might mean we can bring Darcy back home did the job of cheering her up, at least to the point where she stopped trying to be sick and came out of the bathroom. She still looked pale and very frightened, but she was at least able to be productive, and I'm hoping by now that the study is fully clean of any evidence. I'll certainly be checking it when I get home, although nowhere near as thoroughly as a forensic expert with the Chicago police force would be checking it, so she has to have done a perfect job should they ever come to investigate one day.

But while I was able to offer a few words to improve Mom's mood, I haven't been able to find any to make Dad feel better about what has happened tonight. He heard what I said to Mom about Darcy possibly coming home, if I can arrange for such a thing when the time is right, but he didn't smile or do anything that told me he felt my decisive action with Eden was warranted. He's been very quiet, which I hate, because that only makes me think of all the awful things he might be thinking about me since we left the house and drove here.

Darcy and I might have been ruining our own lives on the night she killed Laurence and I decided to hide him here, but now Mom and Dad's lives could be ruined too. Maybe the reason I haven't said anything to him yet is because there is no need to speak when the stakes are so obviously high.

If any one of the four of us gets caught, we'll all end up behind bars, and that will be the lasting legacy of our family.

I want to get back in the car and get going now, not just because it's grim or risky to linger here for too long, but because it's getting colder by the minute as a long night lies ahead. But there's no point getting into the vehicle without Dad – he's the driver and, so far, he hasn't moved a muscle since we got rid of Eden, or at least got rid of her from land anyway.

I'd say my father has gone into shock, but even though I'm a trained medical professional, I don't have the capabilities to bring him out of it. There's nothing I can do to make him better. In fact, my presence here might be making him worse.

'This will only have been worth it if Darcy comes back,' he says, shattering the silence and speaking through his shock.

'Yes, of course,' I say, relieved that Dad is talking again. That has to be a positive sign.

'So you think you can get her to come back?' he asks me seriously.

'Yes,' I reply, faking confidence to hopefully make up for what I currently lack. 'I'll write to her and I'll go down to Florida myself. But I will get her to come home.'

'Unless she's better off without us,' Dad suggests, which sounds less positive.

'What do you mean?'

'Look at what we've done. You, your mother and me. We've done an awful thing here tonight and we're all as guilty as each other. In an attempt to protect our daughter, we have taken somebody else's. Is that right or fair? I don't think so.'

'You can't think like that,' I urge my father. 'Nor should you. What you need to think about is Eden was prepared to let Darcy die. She and Laurence were dangerous, but Darcy survived, and we've helped finish what she started. None of us wanted this, but this is just what happened. We're not the bad guys here.'

'So they are?' Dad asks, nodding to the lake and the two people at the bottom of it.

'Yes,' I say defiantly. 'They are.'

With that, I head for the car. Dad lingers by the lake, but he eventually follows me. Once we're in our seats, he starts the engine and we are on the move. We're heading home to see Mom, to check on the status of her part of the clean-up operation, and to eventually get to the point where we can all get some sleep this evening. I know I'll have to go back to my own house soon, where my husband and son are, and somehow I'll have to act as if everything is okay.

'Is it possible?' Dad asks me now as he drives. 'To carry on in life with the knowledge of what we've done?'

'We have two choices,' I reply as I stare out of the window at the eerie darkness surrounding the huge lake we're leaving behind. 'We either keep our family together and keep our secret, or the world finds out what we did, and we never see each other again.'

'I guess that settles it then,' Dad says with a sad nod of the head and, just like that, we drop the topic and make the rest of the journey in silence.

When we get back to the house, we find Mom sitting in the kitchen, a mop bucket nearby and a blank expression on her face.

We all look at each other and know what needs to happen next.

We need to pray that Eden's body is not found.

We could leave the city while we nervously allow a few days to pass, just in case the police come, but that would require me making up a story to tell Karl and I've lied to my husband more than enough. I also don't want to take Campbell out of kindergarten if I don't have to, because I don't want to mess with his routine and cause issues there either. We might not need to leave anyway, so why cause all that upheaval if the police are never going to suspect us of anything?

So we'll stay.

If enough time passes, then, and only then, is there a chance that the missing fourth member of our family can join us again.

We all miss Darcy.

But after tonight, we might just be closer to getting her back.

TWENTY-ONE

DARCY

'Ten points! Wow, that's a good one!'

I'm impressed with Joe's Scrabble skills as he takes yet another leap ahead of me in our current game, which is our third of the day, not that I'm growing bored of playing yet. As well as Scrabble, we've completed a jigsaw and attempted a few Sudoku puzzles, and our morning of games has certainly been a fun way to pass a few hours. During the games, Joe has mostly been okay, barring one moment where he asked me what time his late wife would be joining us. But apart from that, his memory has been serving him well, certainly well enough to recall all sorts of long words that are getting extra Scrabble points.

'I thought you'd be good at this,' he teases me once he's won another game, and I just shrug my shoulders – there hasn't been much I could do to beat Joe. I was worried that he might be thinking that I was letting him win, something that I bet a man as proud as him would hate to happen, but I think he's realised by now that I'm trying my best and he is simply too good for me.

'Another game?' I suggest after checking the time and seeing that it's not quite noon, so I won't start making lunch yet. But

Joe gets up from his seat, suggesting to me that he has another idea. However, when I hear it, I'm not so sure.

'I was thinking of going for a walk,' he says as he goes and takes his hat from where it hangs on the stand by the door.

'A walk?' I repeat, instantly on guard – the last time Joe was out for a walk, he disappeared and had to be found. 'It'll be lunchtime soon enough. How about I make us some food?'

'We can get lunch out,' Joe says casually, and I realise he really is set on going, especially now he is putting his shoes on.

I consider calling Parker and checking with him if this is a good idea, but he's probably busy and might not answer. Besides, it won't be a big deal as long as I keep an eye on Joe while we're out. So, not wanting to deprive him of getting some fresh air that might improve his mood, I concede.

'Okay, we'll go for a walk. But I just need to visit the bathroom first,' I say, getting up from my own seat and walking away from the box of Scrabble pieces that have kept us occupied for the last few hours.

I lock the bathroom door behind myself before checking my reflection in the mirror and noticing that I look almost as tired as I did first thing today. That was a few hours ago now, when I woke up and was getting ready to come here. At the time, I was still very much unsure whether I should report for duty. After last night's events at the beach, I'd gone home and written them down on a piece of paper. In particular, I had written the words that Joe had said to me before Parker joined us.

He needs to let her go.

She's in danger.

And now so are you.

I had written them down so that I wouldn't forget them, and I had also written down the names of my family members so I wouldn't forget them either. Aware that my memory has more holes in it than a sieve, I felt it best to note down what I could recall, especially in the absence of my notebook, which I still can't find anywhere. It was Joe's words that were making me reluctant to come here again because reading them repeatedly only strengthened the mystery of them, but I hoped I might get closer to solving that mystery by attending work today. However, that has not happened. When I tried to broach the subject with him during our first game this morning, he instantly shot me down.

'I don't know what you're talking about,' he'd said in response to my enquiry about our private conversation by the sea last night.

'You told me I might be in danger,' I'd reminded him. 'Irene too. You remember, right?'

Joe had simply shaken his head then, which hadn't helped me at all. Just as I was beginning to fear he was deliberately withholding further information from me, I remembered his condition and wondered if that was the reason for him forgetting.

It's hard to push somebody for withholding information, but it's even harder when that somebody has a brain condition affecting their memory, so without knowing the real reason Joe was holding out on me, I had to play it safe and assume he had genuinely forgotten.

Still feeling frustrated about it, I let out a sigh before walking away from the mirror and hurrying up with my business in the bathroom, so as not to keep Joe waiting too long for me. But as I leave the bathroom, I can tell he's been impatient because he doesn't answer me when I ask him where he wants to go for a walk.

'Joe?' I call out, figuring he just didn't hear me. But then I see the balcony doors open and assume he's out there.

Only on closer inspection, the balcony is clear.

If he went out there, he's not there anymore.

'Oh my god, Joe!' I cry as I rush to the edge of the balcony and look over the railing, terrified as to what I might see below me when I look down. What if he fell over the edge? What if he's lying there on the ground with a cracked skull, staring up at me with vacant eyes?

What if he's dead and it happened on my watch?

All the reasons Parker is paying me to watch over his father come flooding into mind as I look down and try to see Joe on the ground – the main one of them being that he could accidentally do something to hurt himself when in the midst of a forgetful state. Most people, barring young children and a select few others, are fully aware of the dangers of falls from height, but what about a man who is no longer as capable as he once was? Has Joe got confused and forgotten how dangerous it could be to fall from a height like this one? If he has, he is almost certainly dead, because it's a long way down. Yet as hard as I look, I cannot see him down there. That is good news, but maybe he's just out of view.

There's only one real way to find out.

I rush out into the corridor, scared of what I might discover when I make it to ground level, aware that I have no choice but to check, and the elevator cannot descend quickly enough as I urge it to get me faster to where I need to be.

My sickened stomach feels like it's doing somersaults as I run from the elevator to the door that leads out to the front of the building, but as I get outside, I don't see anything traumatising. There is certainly no sign of a body, or blood, or horrified passers-by holding hands over their open mouths and wishing they could unsee the scene in front of them.

Everything looks normal.

So where the hell is Joe?

For a split second, I wonder if he could still be in his apartment. Maybe I missed him somehow. Maybe he did hear my calls and chose to ignore me. Maybe he is safe and well after all and this stress has been for nothing. But just before I can rush back up to the fifth floor to check, I hear a voice behind me.

'There you are. I thought you'd forgotten to come.'

I spin around and see Joe standing there, his hat on and a smile on his face. Then he extends a hand to me as if to invite me to join him on the walk he has planned all along.

'Oh my god! You're okay? I thought you'd fallen from your balcony!' I cry, all the tension leaving my body now I can relax again.

'I wouldn't say I'm okay, but I'm surviving,' Joe tells me before I take his hand and we start walking.

My heart is still beating a little faster than it should be as we begin our walk, Joe leading me in a different direction along the beach than the one we were in last night. As we go, he points out a few things, including certain bars he liked to have a drink in, as well as a few shops his late wife frequented, but it's the seafood restaurant towards the end of the beachfront that really has him reminiscing.

'We used to eat in there all the time,' Joe says as we stop and look at the restaurant. 'She loved it in there. We both did. So many hours spent just talking. It's full of kids staring at their phones now, but back then, it was quieter and some afternoons it was just us. Chatting. Watching the world go by. Happy to be exactly where we were.'

Joe has tears in his eyes, but when he mentions his late wife again, he's not sad about what he's saying.

'At least she died before she saw what he could be like.'

'Excuse me?' I say, unsure what Joe is trying to tell me.

'Parker. I'm so glad she never got to see the things her son was capable of.'

I quickly realise we're back on the mysterious subject of Parker, and not wanting to miss my chance to learn more before Joe either forgets or pretends to, I press him on it.

'What's so bad about your son?' I ask, getting the feeling I'm finally about to find out.

'I'd rather be in a nursing home than move in with him,' Joe says sharply.

'Parker is saving up for a nursing home for you,' I say, and Joe chuckles.

'He doesn't need to save up. The sale from my apartment alone could more than pay for whatever care I need. He just doesn't want me to go into a home. Not yet anyway. Not until he's sorted out his mess.'

'What mess?'

'His mess at home.'

Joe turns to look back the way we've just come, but I am not ready for us to start walking again, in case this conversation trails off when we move.

'Tell me what's going on with Parker,' I plead. 'It's to do with his girlfriend, right? Irene?'

Joe lets out a sigh and he looks like he might be getting annoyed, but then he speaks again.

'He doesn't want me in a nursing home because he's worried I might talk,' he says.

'Talk about what?'

'About what he's doing.'

'What is he doing?' I ask, impatient, but more than a little scared as well.

'You need to help her,' Joe says quietly, his voice just loud enough to be heard over a distant Jet Ski engine.

'Irene?'

Joe nods.

'Help her how? What's wrong?' I ask, and Joe suddenly looks at me with an expression I haven't seen him wear before.

There's fear on his face.

'You want to know why I'd rather be in a nursing home than live with my son?' Joe asks, his expression only growing worse with each passing second. 'It's because of what he's hiding in his basement.'

TWENTY-TWO

PIPPA

As I look around my basement, I see nothing particularly exciting. Just a washing machine, some bags full of clothes that need to go to a charity shop and a few DIY projects that my husband started but quickly grew bored of. I came down here to check on the status of my laundry, but if I'm honest, I also came down here because I needed a break from being around the people upstairs.

Karl and Campbell, my husband and son, are both as demanding on my time as ever, and each in their own individual ways. Karl is still in a bad mood with me, still holding back from being the good partner I need him to be, because he still thinks I'm holding back on telling him what is really on my mind. I miss the couple we used to be, the ones who told each other everything because we had trust. Unfortunately, my husband is right, of course. I am holding back. I'm holding back a lot, but if he knew, I think he'd prefer it if I didn't divulge what was really on my mind. If I did, he'd have to hear about the two bodies I put in Lake Michigan, and about how I beat one of those people over the head with a lamp, and the final cherry on top would be telling him that Darcy left because she's killed someone too.

How's that for an update, hubs? Still want me to tell you all my secrets now?

As for my son, he is currently lying in his bed with the flu, an illness that is keeping him out of kindergarten today and also keeping me off work. I can't get childcare, so I told my boss at the hospital that I won't be in today and that is that. At least it means I don't have to deal with the stresses of my workplace with all the things going on in my head right now. As expected, my boss wasn't happy about me not reporting for duty today, but that's perfectly normal for the manager of an understaffed, overpopulated children's ward. I guess it's true that I cannot get childcare, although I didn't actually ask anybody.

I certainly didn't ask my parents.

Figuring that Mom and Dad need some time to themselves to process what has happened recently, I decided not to call them to see if they could come and look after their grandson while Karl and I went to work. It's a typically hectic morning here as Karl prepares to leave for his office and we collectively fight the fatigue from the broken sleep caused by our son's illness. I can't risk my parents having some kind of breakdown with Campbell around, especially when news of that could get back to my husband and give him even more reason to suspect that something is wrong. Much better for me to stay off work and care for my son myself, while I hope that Mom and Dad are taking all the time and privacy they need to cope with what we did together.

Unfortunately, I cannot control how they are choosing to cope, and I have a feeling at least one of my parents will be sat in front of the news channels at home, worried every time a 'breaking news' bulletin pops up on screen and wondering if the police are on the way to arrest them. That wouldn't be a healthy thing for them to be doing, although I couldn't blame them if that's how they're choosing to spend their time; I've certainly been checking the news at regular intervals on my phone in fear of a frightening update from a journalist relating to Lake Michigan and a grim discovery.

I forge on with my chores, taking the opportunity to wash a few of my nurse's uniforms so they're ready for when I return to work. Once the washing cycle has started I head upstairs to check on my son. But on my way to see him, I encounter my husband, who I was hoping would have left for work by now. But he hasn't, and when I see what he is holding, I understand why.

It's a letter.

He must have been leaving just as the postman arrived.

But what is it that's been delivered today?

I know it can't be anything from Darcy. I made sure to give her a PO Box address for any correspondence to me, which allows me to keep all her letters secret from my husband, in case he read one. But as I get closer to him, I see that he is holding a handwritten letter and, shockingly, the handwriting looks like it matches that of my sister's.

But how can that be?

'What's that?' I ask, hoping I'm mistaken, and surely I must be because I didn't give Darcy my home address, and there's no way that she could recall it with her condition. But as Karl sees me coming, he holds up the letter and, strangely, he has a grin on his face.

'It's from Darcy. Quite interesting reading too,' he says rather smugly, and I freeze – a part of my private life that I carefully constructed seems to have just developed a serious crack in it.

'What?' is all I can say in response, but Karl looks like he expected me to be surprised and, even worse, it looks like he's taking pleasure in it.

'What's the matter? I'm just reading a letter from my sister-in-law. She's family, right? It shouldn't be a big deal, should it?

It makes sense that I'd be concerned about her, but now I don't have to be because I've read this.'

Karl sniggers before he tosses the letter onto the kitchen countertop, and I rush to pick it up, fearful of what might be contained within it and how much my husband might know now. I know Darcy should have forgotten everything that happened before she left Chicago because of the injuries to her brain, but what if she's been having flashbacks? What if her memory has returned? And what if she has just written some very incriminating things in her latest letter?

Incriminating for both her and for me.

My eyes scan over the writing as quickly as they can while my brain works overtime to process the words as quickly as possible so I can ascertain just how bad this is. But my reading time is interrupted by my husband sniggering again.

'I knew it. I knew you were hiding something from me, and I knew it had to do with your sister. Well, now I know for sure.'

He knows? Oh my god, what has Darcy written?

'Wait, I can explain!' I cry before I've even finished reading my sister's letter, but I have to do something to slow down my partner, because this could be bad. Really, really bad.

'It sounds like she's been busy,' Karl says as I try to finish reading, and I'm getting a sense of what he means. Darcy has written about a new job she has, something about caring for the dad of some guy she met in a café, but I'm reading so fast, and my heart is pounding so hard and the words on the page are starting to get blurry as I fear my entire world is about to crumble down. But then a strange thing happens. Karl stops interrupting me and I manage to finish reading the letter and, when I do, I see that there is no mention of anything criminal in it.

No words about Laurence and his body or Lake Michigan and my involvement. Nor is there anything about Eden or how me and my sister could both be in serious trouble if she ever went to the police. That's good because it shows my sister's memory has not returned, as expected. It also means my husband still doesn't know the truth of why Darcy left the city and why I've been deliberately distant with him about it. But what is not explained here is how my husband came to be in possession of this letter.

'I don't understand,' I say. 'How did you get this?'

'You're wondering why the letter was sent here and not to that PO Box, aren't you?' Karl says, raising his eyebrows as if he's just let me in on a very clever plot. 'Well, I'll tell you. I knew you were hiding something from me, so I made sure to find out what it might be. That means I've had to do some sneaking and snooping around. I'm talking about your phone, your laptop, your emails, anything I could get my hands on while you were either out of the house or asleep. And I'm sorry, but if that makes me sound like a paranoid husband, then yes, Pippa, that's exactly what I've become, because you've left me with no other choice.'

'You've been looking through my personal things?' I ask, afraid not because it demonstrates a huge lack of trust in our relationship, but rather because he clearly found something he shouldn't have while looking.

'I sure have, and I don't even feel guilty for doing so because of how you've been with me over these last few months,' Karl replies calmly, not a hint of regret on his face or in his voice. 'I knew you were hiding something and you were. You were hiding a PO Box address. I found it saved in a note on your phone, and once I found out it was registered to you, I was able to pose as you and reroute any mail to it. I re-routed it right here, which is why this letter arrived today.'

It's a lot to take in, but I don't have time to process any of it. I could go into damage limitation mode and explain why there was the need for a secret mailing address for my sister, but something tells me that, unless I'm fully truthful, Karl won't believe me and that will only make things worse. That's why I opt for a different strategy, perhaps an even riskier one, at least as far as the future of my relationship is concerned.

'I can't believe you did this! It's totally unacceptable to go through my things behind my back. I'm disgusted at you.'

That's it. That's the strategy. Turn this back onto my husband. Make out like he's the bad guy here and not me, even though I know I have to take my fair share of blame for driving him to this point in the first place. The problem with this strategy is that it's only going to make our arguing worse, and the way things are headed now, our relationship is breaking beyond repair.

It's merciful then that before either of us can say another word, we hear Campbell calling us from upstairs. No matter what we might be arguing about, Karl and I will always put aside our issues when our son needs us, and as he's currently ill, we move to respond to him even quicker than usual.

'I'll go,' I say as I head for the stairs, and I'm hoping that Karl is going to say he's going to work and we can put this conversation on hold until he gets back this evening. But he doesn't do that and chooses to follow me upstairs instead, much to my disappointment. Maybe he's not even planning to go to work at all today, which would be really problematic. I don't want him here for the next several hours to prolong this painful state of affairs. I don't say a word to him as we head for Campbell's bedroom, and he doesn't say a word either.

I enter our son's bedroom first, but surprisingly there's no sign of him. He's not in his bed lying underneath his comforter where I left him, but his voice definitely came from up here, so he has to be around somewhere. Then I hear what sounds like the television and I know exactly where he is. Karl is already on the same wavelength as me, at least when it comes to our child and his mischievous movements, and as we enter our bedroom we see Campbell lying on our bed with a remote control in his hand.

I should have known he'd try this trick at some point today. There's no television in his bedroom but there is one in ours, and that's why the supposedly sickly little boy has made the short journey from his bed to ours.

'You're supposed to be resting, buddy,' Karl says as he takes a seat on the edge of the bed beside Campbell. He's clearly not mad at our son. I'm not mad either – this is actually a welcome distraction from what was going on downstairs, but that's only until I see what it is that Campbell has been watching.

It's the news, and now I realise what has got him so excited. It's all the people wearing the familiar uniform, the one he loves so much whenever we see it when we're out around the city.

'Police!' Campbell cries, pointing to the screen as if we need any more clue to as to what he means, but Karl and I both know what the police look like, and we can see that there are certainly plenty of them on this news bulletin. But that's not all there is.

There's something else too, and when I see what it is, I could collapse onto the floor and stop breathing.

It's a lake.

I don't need a geography expert to tell me which lake it is. It's the closest one to our house and by far the biggest. It's a lake that is known all around the world.

And it's the lake I was at last night with my father.

It's taking all my energy to not start hyperventilating, but my breathing is getting shallower by the second, and the precious oxygen my body needs to function is in increasingly short supply as I stare at the TV in terror.

Campbell continues to get excited about all the police on screen while Karl is intrigued as to what the boat out on the water is doing. That's certainly what the reporter seems to be focusing on too. The boat is the important thing here because, apparently, there's something in the water that warrants further investigation.

Something has been found.

I don't need the reporter to tell me that it's a body.

I figured that from how many police officers there are by the shore.

The only thing I don't know is whose body it is.

TWENTY-THREE

DARCY

It's always nice to receive a handful of cash after a long day's work. But the excitement is tempered somewhat by the fact that I don't know if I can trust the person paying me.

'Thanks for your help today,' Parker says with a smile. 'Same time again tomorrow?'

'Yeah, of course,' I say, not wanting to reply with anything that might make Parker feel something is wrong. But there is something wrong, seriously wrong, and I've decided that I'm going to try and find out what it is tonight.

The normal plan for me now would be to leave Joe's place and head back to my own apartment and, ultimately, try and get some sleep as the day winds down to a close. But I'm not going to do that. Instead, I'm going to investigate the claims that Joe made to me earlier today when we were out for a walk and he said some very unsettling things.

He was talking about Irene, Parker's girlfriend, and how I needed to help her. He also mentioned that there was something in Parker's basement that warranted attention. But he didn't tell me any more, possibly because he doesn't know much else, or maybe because he's too afraid to utter it. But he certainly told me enough for me to know what I have to do.

I have to follow Parker home tonight and find out where he lives.

Then I have to try and see what he's hiding.

I intend to do that, but I can't let Parker know, so I have to make everything seem like it is fine.

'Thank you,' I say to him as I put the money in my purse, before turning to his father who sits in the armchair in front of the television, watching another baseball game. 'I'll see you tomorrow, Joe.'

Joe doesn't turn to look at me before I leave, choosing instead to lift a hand in the air in acknowledgement, but that's fine because I know he's engrossed in the game. Or maybe it's just because he's already said enough to me today and that took a lot for him to do, so he's reverting back to being quieter now his work is done.

'Have a good evening,' Parker says to me as I leave the apartment, but he has no clue what I really intend to do tonight.

As I get into the elevator and head down to ground level, not even I know the full itinerary for the rest of my day. My plan is to find a hiding spot outside this apartment building and wait to see if Parker leaves. I guess he will eventually, when his father is in bed, which could be a while, but I'm prepared to wait. When he does leave, I will follow him, tailing him all the way back to his own home and then I'll see what is waiting for me there.

As I leave the building and find myself what seems like a perfectly good hiding place behind several very large palm tree trunks in the gardens nearby, I wish Joe had just given me his son's address so I could have gone there straight away. I did ask him for Parker's residence, but he wouldn't give it to me, saying that I should just forget what he told me and leave it. But that was a ridiculous suggestion because how could I *just forget* it? It was obviously important, or he wouldn't have told me there was something wrong in the first place. But it doesn't matter. I'm going to find out what is really going on here and nothing can stop me now.

I remain in my hiding place behind the palm trees as the sky turns from blue to pink and, eventually, to an inky black. It would have been quite a spectacular sunset to witness from the beach, but I didn't get to see the full show here – I have more important things to do than hang out on the sand with tourists and locals. I am waiting to see Parker walk out of the building opposite me and, as soon as I do, I'll be giving chase.

To pass the time, I think about what Parker is probably doing up on the fifth floor in his father's apartment. Possibly making him his evening meal or helping him shower. Maybe he's watching the ball game with him or perhaps the Scrabble board has come out again. Whatever it is, it's all time that I have to while away here, nothing to distract myself with except my own imagination, which is more than prone to running wild the longer it is left unchecked. But then, shortly after eight in the evening, I see the building door open and a handsome man steps out. It's Parker, and as he turns left and starts walking at a brisk pace, I step out from behind the palm tree and follow him, having to keep a safe distance because I don't have a hood or anything to disguise my appearance. It's usually a good thing that the climate here is warm enough to never warrant a coat, but I wish I was wearing one right now so I could put a hood over my head and make my face less visible.

I have to walk faster than I anticipated, while ensuring I remain far enough away not to be noticed, because Parker is certainly in a hurry. I presume he's trying to get home as quickly as he can to salvage what is left of his evening, having spent a large part of it looking after his father. If he is going home at all. He could be going somewhere else. To a restaurant or a bar, maybe. That would not help me because I'd have to wait outside for him again. But whatever he is doing, he has to go home at some point, and when he does, I'll be right behind him.

I keep my distance as we walk. We're moving parallel to the beach, though we're not by the sand and the people. We're one street back from that, so there are rows of high-rise buildings separating us from the ocean, and I wonder why Parker has opted for this route rather than the more scenic one.

Maybe it's quicker.

Or maybe he wants to be seen by fewer people.

Fortunately, there are still enough people on the sidewalk to make it less obvious that I'm following him were he to look back over his shoulder, not that he has so far. There's no way he should suspect me of still being here now. He sent me home hours ago. He's probably not even thinking about me at all.

But all I'm thinking about is him.

We keep walking for fifteen minutes. The high-rise apartments become fewer and we enter a neighbourhood that looks very different to the end of the beach where I live. Unlike my area, which is built up and crowded, not to mention overpopulated with shops, cafés and bars, this place seems much quieter and more exclusive. Instead of apartment blocks, there are whitewashed homes, and the further we go the more the homes become mansions, sprawling lawns behind tall gates and sports cars parked in front of the kind of houses only the wealthiest people in the state could afford.

What is Parker doing here?

I see him stop suddenly outside one property and, as he lingers by the gate, I'm expecting him to press the intercom buzzer to alert whoever owns this huge house that he is here and they should let him in. But that doesn't happen. Instead of ringing for permission to access, he simply enters a keycode and the gates swing open on command, allowing him to stride up the driveway in the direction of the massive property.

What is this?

Is this where Parker lives?

It can't be. He's told me he is saving up to put his father into a nursing home, so I figured money was tight. But this does not look like the kind of place a person struggling for cash would live. But there's not much time for me to ponder this further because I have a problem. The gates are starting to close again and in a few seconds they'll be sealed and locked and only a keycode that I don't have will be able to open them again.

If I want to get inside and get a closer look at where Parker lives, I need to get beyond those gates before they close.

So I start running, my feet padding on the hot blacktop as I approach the gate, and I'm hoping that Parker is far enough ahead of me not to hear me approaching quickly.

The gates are almost closed now, but I quicken my pace and, somehow, just make it through them before they shut behind me. Then I dart behind the nearest bush and crouch down before peeping my head back up, checking to see if Parker saw me. But he didn't. He's simply unlocking his front door and going inside.

I made it onto his property, technically, though it's not the kind of property I was expecting.

So what else about Parker is going to surprise me?

TWENTY-FOUR

PIPPA

I don't know how I did it, but I somehow managed it.

I managed to not lose my mind in front of my family when the news came through that a body had been found in Lake Michigan.

Despite the fear I felt when I saw what was happening in the news report that Campbell had been watching on the TV in our bedroom, I was able to remain calm enough to not give away the fact that I was falling apart inside. I guess I had no other choice. If I'd given anything away then Karl would have surely noticed and that would have been disastrous. He'd already been asking me enough questions as it was after finding out about the PO Box and Darcy's letter. But that was okay. That could be somewhat contained.

What could not be contained would be him knowing that I put that body in the lake.

Not knowing whose body it is that has been found does not change the fact that I put it there. Whether it's Laurence or Eden, I was the last person to see either of them before they went into the water, but I'm not the last person to see either of them now one of them has been found. Whoever it is, him or her, they will be looked at by numerous people. Forensic experts, detectives, police officers, recovery crews, possibly even some journalists if they're daring enough to get that close to the crime scene. There may even be a member of the public or two who get to catch a glimpse of the corpse, though they'll probably wish they hadn't tried if they do, such is the lasting effect it will likely have on them.

All I am waiting for now is for the news to report exactly who has been found. The gender of the body has not been revealed yet, not that I'll feel any better when it is because it's still terrible news. Those bodies were supposed to stay hidden at the bottom of the lake forever.

This was not part of the plan at all.

Despite things clearly going awry, I kept my emotions in check while my husband was still in the house. I knew he had to go to work at some point, so I turned off the television, told Campbell he was to get back in his own bed and then told Karl that we would talk about all the things we needed to later tonight. Thankfully, and possibly just because he didn't want to get in trouble with his employer, Karl went along with that plan, and by the time Campbell was in his own bed again, my husband had left the house. That gave me some much-needed breathing space to process the frightening news bulletin, although it came with a very heavy moment. As I was tucking my son in, I was struck by the awful thought that it might be the last time I ever get to do such a simple thing as get him settled on his pillow. The last time I ever get to care for him while he's sick. The last time I get to see him as a cute little four-year-old who needs me more than anyone else in the world.

I needed to push those thoughts out of my head as quickly as I could, so after leaving my son to nap, I went straight downstairs to turn the TV on and keep tabs on the news.

That's what I've been doing ever since.

There's still no word on who has been found in the lake, but every media outlet in Chicago has jumped on this and speculation is rife. It hasn't taken long for people to wonder if the body belongs to Laurence, the missing man who has been in the headlines enough already over the past few months. Some are suggesting it could be Eden, which also might be true, though I am glad a few people are wondering if it is somebody else, somebody entirely unconnected, and I guess I'm hoping that too. There is a small chance that this body has nothing to do with me. I don't know how many other homicides there have been in Chicago, but surely I can't be the first person to ever choose the huge lake beside our city to hide a body. Maybe it's a body from years ago. Maybe it's connected to the mobsters of the past, like something out of a gangster movie. It could just be something to do with a plain old domestic dispute between a husband and wife and one of them wound up dead.

Or maybe I'm not that lucky.

Maybe this has my fingerprints all over it.

As I keep watching, the only new thing I learn is that a body was found by a fisherman, who was out in his small vessel at dawn and came across something sticking out of the water. Apparently, the body, whoever it is, was found stuck in a clump of reeds, meaning it was visible rather than unseen in the murky depths.

If it's Laurence then his body must have floated up somehow.

If it's Eden, I guess her body never really went down like I thought it did.

If it's anybody else, I'll be the happiest woman in Chicago.

I'm going through a rollercoaster of emotions as I wait for news, a rollercoaster I was initially sent on all because I tried to help my sister. Now I fear this rollercoaster is out of control, but the brakes came off the moment I realised Darcy needed me to do whatever it took to keep her safe.

The obvious thing for me to do would be to call my parents

and tell them not to panic. But I haven't done that so far, for a couple of reasons. One, I'm hoping that, somehow, they haven't turned on the news today and therefore have no idea that Lake Michigan is currently an active crime scene. Two, I feel like it would be pointless for us to have a conversation in which I tell them not to panic, because if they have heard this news, there's no way they will be staying calm. Mom will probably be drinking again, if she isn't doing that anyway, while Dad will either be in a silent spiral of despair or telling me we need to call a lawyer, which would be a bad idea unless the police have arrived. But so far there are no police. Not here, and I'm guessing not at Mom and Dad's either, so everything is okay, for now at least.

But the clock is ticking and, as if I didn't have enough problems, I know Karl will be home from work soon. When he is, not only will he want to pick up the conversation about Darcy and what might be going on with her, but I'll have to put on my act like everything is fine and the news isn't bothering me. If only I could stay here, in a room on my own, I feel like I could control this. But that's not realistic. I live with other people, plus there are others outside of this house who can get in the way of things too.

Families.

Why do they always complicate things?

I can hear Campbell calling me again. He probably wants food or a drink or maybe he wants to watch TV. Looking after him could be a welcome distraction, except it's not. That's because every time I look at my son's face, I am reminded of what I stand to lose if the truth comes out about what I've done. If I go to prison, I won't see his face for a very long time or, if I do, it'll only be because somebody has had to bring him to visit me in whatever awful place I'm residing. He'll be confused why Mommy is wearing a uniform. He'll ask why I'm surrounded by officers with handcuffs and guns. Most of all, he'll want to know why I can't just come home with him.

It breaks my heart to think about being separated from my son forever, but that's what will happen if this situation gets out of hand. Maybe it's already too late, but I have to pray that it's not. I also have to pray that somehow, without expressly telling him the problem, I can convince my husband to forget his paranoia and his obsession with finding out every single detail about Darcy. I need him to drop it – he cannot know the truth.

He can't know because I might not be able to trust him to keep it quiet. He already told me the trust has gone from our relationship. So that's all I need to know to tell me that he would not be on my side if the worst was to happen and the police were to come to our door.

TWENTY-FIVE

DARCY

My heart rate increases when a large security light comes on above Parker's entrance, illuminating the part of the driveway that I thought I was stealthily sneaking up. Desperate for darkness again, I race to the side of the house and press my back against the wall, trying to get my breathing back under control before making my next move.

Parker is inside his house now, while I'm stuck outside it, but that doesn't mean I shouldn't be able to see what is going on in there. I'll have to be quiet, and very careful, but I am hoping I can peer through a few windows and get more of an insight into what he might be hiding inside.

If he's hiding anything at all, that is.

I'm well aware that I'm here because I'm trusting the word of a man with a serious brain condition, which means he might not be the most reliable of narrators, but something makes me think that Joe is telling the truth. If it's motivated me to be here, risking not only Parker seeing me and firing me immediately, but also risking him calling the police, I guess I believe there is truth to what Joe said. That means I'm looking for two things here.

Parker's girlfriend, Irene.

And that basement.

The security light goes off again, and it's a relief not to have my surroundings flooded with a bright yellow beam that was only making my task harder. Now it's dark again, I feel more confident to move, so I creep down the side of the house and make my way to the first window.

Peeping inside and praying that Parker is not going to be looking out at the same time, I see a large hallway with a curving marble staircase and several paintings on the wall. This house is even dreamier on the inside than it is on the outside, and I'm once again struck by how jarring this is. A man who lives here could surely afford whatever he needed, so why did Parker make out like paying for professional care for his father was beyond his reach? I'm no art dealer, but by the looks of some of those paintings near the stairs, I'm guessing the sale of a couple of those could get Joe some first-class care in one of the area's best nursing homes for at least a year or two. But, for whatever reason, Parker has been lying to me, and I'm guessing the extent of his lies goes far beyond what he's already told me, so I have to keep investigating.

Moving on to the next window, I look inside and see a dining room, the kind any host would love to entertain dinner guests in. There are eight chairs sitting around an oval-shaped table that could easily fit all manner of exquisite dishes and expensive glasses of wine, though currently there is only a set of candlesticks in the centre of it. Parker is not in here, nor is anybody else, so I guess I should move on again.

I reach a third window, but that only allows me to look into a pantry where I see dozens of shelves stocked with all sorts of spices. I'm still no nearer to finding the homeowner or anybody else who might be in there, so I forge on, and now I'm at the rear of the property. I gasp when I see the backyard – if I thought the front was impressive then this is something else entirely.

The lawn seems to stretch impossibly away from me, so much so that I cannot even see the back boundary where it might end. My view is not only hindered by the dark but by the ominous silhouette of the oak tree that stands proudly in the centre of the lawn. It's looking a little spooky at this time of day, with the wind blowing gently through its leaves, but I imagine it looks spectacular when the sun is up and this garden is full of people enjoying a barbecue in the shade of its impressive branches. But all is quiet tonight, and while I'm worrying that another security light is going to come on as soon as I start stepping across the patio, I'm thankful when it does not.

Still in darkness, I creep to the nearest window, and I see that it offers me a view of a kitchen.

I also see that Parker is standing right in the middle of it.

The man I followed here is surrounded by gleaming countertops, shiny pots and pans hanging from sharp hooks and almost enough appliances to fill an aisle in a department store. I watch as he moves past the coffee machine on his way to the microwave, where he opens the door and takes out a steaming packet of rice. I see him tip the rice onto a plate before he opens a tin of tomatoes and puts a few of them on top. It looks like a very basic meal, surely one very undeserving of a kitchen like this one, but maybe Parker is just tired and cannot be bothered to cook. Or maybe his personal chef went home hours ago, because if he lives here he can certainly afford one. But perhaps there's another reason for the very meagre meal that has just been prepared.

Perhaps it's not for Parker at all.

I start to wonder if that is the case when I see the man of the house snacking on some candy, the food he just made sitting untouched on the counter nearby. He doesn't look like he's going to sit down and tuck into the meal, but if he's not eating it, who is?

I can't see anybody else in there with him, and I'm tempted

to try another window to see if I might spot someone, but just before I can do that Parker stops snacking and picks up the plate again. Then he carries it to a closed door, takes a key off a hook and slides it into the lock.

He turns the key and the door opens, which just leaves me to watch as Parker enters the mysterious room with the food before the door closes behind him.

Where has he gone? What's in there?

Why was that door locked?

I have lots of questions, but I can't get any answers from my current vantage point. It's not like moving will help me either, because whatever room that door leads to, it's in the centre of this house, so there won't be any windows that show me inside it anyway. I guess I'm stuck here until Parker comes back out, but how long will that be?

I decide to move on to the next window while I wait, just to see if there's anything of interest in there. I see into a lounge. There's a large and very comfortable-looking sofa sitting directly in front of a huge TV, and it looks like the perfect place to sprawl out and watch a show in the evening after a hard day's work. I can just imagine myself lying there, relaxing, and watching something that helps take my mind off all my daily stresses.

Then something weird happens.

Even though this lounge is empty, I suddenly imagine two people sitting there, as if I'm having a vision of them, or maybe it's something else.

Maybe it's a flashback.

A man and woman, clearly a couple judging by how close they are to one another, sit together on the sofa, sharing a bowl of snacks and enjoying a glass of red wine while watching television. I feel like I've seen these people before. I know them from somewhere. But who are they?

Are they the people from my notebook?

Are they my parents?

Aware that this must be some kind of memory, I try to recall a time in the past when I was sneaking around a house and peering in through the windows at night. But as always with my brain, anything that happened a long time ago has gone – left in as much darkness and uncertainty as those shadows in the yard behind me.

This flashback has made me very unsettled, and I feel like I need to get out of here – I'm not in the right frame of mind to be doing something as risky as this. That's why I choose to head back the way I came, heading for the kitchen window, and beyond that will be my escape route down the side of the house and over the front gate to the freedom of the streets beyond. But I'm not paying attention and taking as much care as I was earlier and that's why, as I pass the kitchen window, I'm not careful in trying to stay out of sight.

It's why, when I glance inside, I see Parker standing right there.

And he sees me.

I scream when I realise that I've been caught, and my next reaction is to start running. He might have just caught me sneaking around outside his house, but it could be worse.

He could physically catch me.

I'm not prepared to let that happen so I run as fast as I can and, as I round the side of the house, I'm really picking up speed. I'm just hoping it's enough to beat Parker, who is surely racing to the front of his house too, hoping to catch me before I make it over his gate. But before I can even get to his driveway and activate the security light there, my right foot thuds into something hard. It could be a tree stump, or it could be a garden tool, but whatever it is, it's surprised me and knocked me off balance, and now my momentum is sending me tumbling to the ground.

I groan as my body hits the soil beside the path that I was

running around, but I really let out a loud noise when my head thumps into something harder behind me. I think my skull just clipped a tree trunk as I fell, but I'm far too dazed to check what it was, and it's taking all my energy just to put a hand to my head and feel the throbbing.

'Urgh,' is all I can muster as I try to regain my bearings and stop the pounding in my head, but I took quite a hit and now I'm feeling nauseous. But I feel even worse when I hear footsteps approaching me, and despite trying to get to my feet before the person reaches me, I fail to do so.

I'm lying on the ground, on my back, in the dark and with a bad head injury.

Just before I pass out, I see the person standing over me.

Parker.

TWENTY-SIX

PIPPA

'Campbell, please. Put that down. I'm not going to tell you again.'

My frustration with my supposedly sick child has been growing stronger all day and into the evening, and I don't care what he says, tomorrow he is going back to kindergarten because there's clearly nothing wrong with him. Of course, my mood has not been helped by the gnawing paranoia I've had to endure ever since I saw the news report, and I've been keeping tabs on the news ever since, which hasn't been easy with Campbell running around the house at the same time.

'Campbell! Stop it!' I cry, totally exasperated, and the volume of my voice gets my son's attention, and he mercifully stops doing what he shouldn't be doing and comes to a halt, out of breath but with a mischievous grin on his face that tells me he's not quite done yet. I need him to calm down, or at least I need his father to get home and give me some help with him. But there's no sign of Karl yet, even though it's past the time when he's usually getting in from work, so I'm still very much on my own here.

'Any more messing around and you'll be going straight to

bed without your dinner!' I say to Campbell, who thinks about that for a minute before deciding he would like some food so he better stop testing me.

'Why don't you go and play with your toys in the playroom, and I'll be in in a minute,' I suggest, feeling guilty as I see his little body slinking away to do as I say.

Now he's out of the way, I can make another quick check on the news, so I turn the TV back on and see what updates might be waiting for me. But all the channels are on commercial breaks, so I'll have to wait a few more minutes before the bulletins are back on.

I'm about to go and see what we have in the fridge for dinner, because if my son isn't asking me for food soon, my husband probably will be, but before I get there, I check my phone, which I haven't done for a few hours. It's been lying on the table in the hallway, and I've barely had a chance to look at it, as Campbell has been keeping me busy, but when I look I see several missed calls from Dad.

Oh no. What's happened now?

I need to call him back, but just before I can do that the landline rings and I go to grab it from its holder, which is located in the hallway too, at the bottom of the stairs as that's the most convenient place to keep the communal phone. But the holder is empty, which means whoever used it last did not replace it on the charger.

I bet that was Karl. I always put it back where it belongs when I'm finished with it, but now that it's not there, I have to go hunting for it around the house. I can still hear the phone ringing as I begin my search. If I don't find it quickly enough, the call will go to voicemail. Then the ringing stops.

Has the caller hung up?

It's not the end of the world if they have, and it's not as if I'm not busy enough without having an extra thing to add to the list, but then I hear Campbell's voice coming from the playroom. It sounds like he's talking to somebody, and when I walk in I see that he has the phone and is chattering away to whoever is at the other end of the line.

'Who's that?' I ask him, nervous. Having been on edge all day I'm starting to become fearful of everything, including a simple call to the house.

'It's Grandpa!' Campbell cries excitedly, and while I'm relieved it's no one more sinister, like a detective looking for me or Darcy, I can't relax as I have a feeling I know why my father is calling here. He wants to talk about what's happening on the news and, because I haven't been answering my phone, he's had no choice but to call the house.

'Give me the phone,' I say urgently to my son, clicking my fingers to get his attention when he turns his back on me to keep talking to his grandfather.

'I've been at home all day today, Grandpa!' Campbell says to my father as he continues to keep the phone out of my reach, moving around the playroom so that I can't catch up with him.

'Campbell, give me the phone, please. I'm not going to ask you again,' I say, my frustration levels rising rapidly once more and threatening to become unmanageable. But that still doesn't work and, as my son continues to defy me, I lose my temper. The eruption that has been threatening all day is now ready to be unleashed on the smallest person in this house.

'GIVE ME THAT DAMN PHONE NOW!' I shout at the top of my voice, and Campbell instantly drops it, such is the level of his shock. Then he starts crying. I feel bad for upsetting him, but I'm so frazzled that I don't know what to say to comfort him, and I haven't even got to hear what Dad has to say yet. This conversation is best to be had out of earshot of my son, in case he passes on details of it to his father when he gets home, so I give Campbell a quick hug – another possible 'last' – before I leave the playroom with the phone pressed to my ear.

'Dad. I've seen the news, and you need to stay calm. Everything's going to be okay,' I tell him as I can hear my son's sobs softening in the playroom.

'Stay calm! How can you say that? They've found her!' he cries, and now he's the one giving me news.

'What?'

'Eden! It's her body they've found in the lake!'

Dad's panicked voice shoots down the phone line, enters my ear and goes right into my brain, and now I'm as stressed as he is. I need extra confirmation, so I reach the TV in the lounge and, when I do, I see that he is correct. The news is reporting that the body pulled from the lake this morning is that of a female, and while she has not been named yet, we already know her identity.

'I thought you said that was a good place to put her,' Dad cries. 'I thought you said we could get away with this!'

Dad's words are just noise in my head now, as are Campbell's as he enters the lounge, still crying, before telling me that I am a naughty mom for shouting at him.

This is sensory overload, but I really need to hear the news report, so I turn up the volume and, as I try to listen to the latest update on the investigation, I see images of more divers searching around the lake.

Why are they still looking in the water?

Why haven't they stopped and gone home now the body has been found?

What if they keep looking and find the other one?

'Pippa! What do we do?' Dad begs, making me feel like the parent and him the child. 'Your mother is in tears in the kitchen. She's already drunk a bottle of wine. I think she's having a nervous breakdown and I'm not far behind her.'

Dad is losing it, Mom sounds like she's already way ahead of him, and now Campbell is tugging at my sweatshirt to get my attention.

'Mommy, I'm sorry!!' Campbell keeps crying, tears running down his cheeks. 'Mommy!'

'Stop!' I shout at the top of my voice, not to anyone in particular, but to everybody who is bothering me at the moment. I guess that would be my father on the phone, my son beside me and even the reporter on the TV, even though they can't hear me. The reporter is the only one who doesn't go quiet, but Dad and Campbell do. For a brief second, I have a moment of peace. But that is shattered when I hear the voice behind me.

'Pippa? What the hell is going on?'

I turn around and see Karl in the doorway. I guess I didn't hear him come in, but that's hardly a surprise with all the noise a moment ago. But he is here, and it seems he heard me and my outburst, given the grave look of concern on his face.

'Daddy!' Campbell cries, and he runs towards his father, needing some comfort from at least one parent. I feel terrible for not being the one to provide it. I also feel awful for losing my temper with him in the first place, and I go to apologise but Karl shields our child from me, which is like a dagger to my heart.

'I'm sorry,' I try lamely, and Campbell doesn't look at me, while I wish Karl wouldn't because his eyes are boring into me, and he's clearly disgusted to have walked in on such a scene as he did a few seconds ago. Neither my son nor my husband seem to recognise me, and why should they? I'm normally calm and collected, loving and loyal, yet I'm all over the place, losing my temper as easily as I feel like I'll soon be losing my family and my freedom.

Dad is still on the phone, and I can hear him asking me what we do, while the television is still blaring, and now Karl is paying attention to what the reporter is saying, meaning it's not going to take too long for him to make the connection between my distressed emotional state and the content of the report.

Sure enough, he figures it out and, after grabbing the remote control and turning the TV off, he tells me to hang up the phone. I feel bad cutting Dad off, but I do so anyway, and after Karl has told Campbell to go into the playroom for a minute, the house is suddenly silent.

'This is it, Pippa,' my husband says to me calmly and clearly as tears run down my cheeks. 'You tell me what is going on right now or me and Campbell are out of here. And don't even lie to me, because I'm guessing it's bad. It's got something to do with what's going on at the lake, hasn't it? It's got something to do with Darcy too, right? So start talking. Or this marriage is over. More importantly, your relationship with your son is over too.'

TWENTY-SEVEN

DARCY

I see myself in a hospital, a nurse's uniform on and patients all around me, begging for help, begging me to tend to them next. But I can't help them. I can't help any of them. That's because, despite their problems, I'm the one who needs help the most. I'm in danger. I'm being chased through the corridors. Somebody wants to hurt me. But I can't get away.

I've run into a dead end.

When I turn around, I know there is no escape.

My eyes open and I realise that was a bad dream. But the nightmare doesn't end when I remember where I am and what happened just before I lost consciousness. I see Parker standing in front of me and I can feel my head throbbing. That's right. I was spying on him, and he caught me, and in my desperation to get away I fell and hit my head – and now I'm here.

Inside his house.

He's blocking the exit.

Just like in my dream, I'm trapped.

'Welcome back,' Parker says with a sly smile. 'I was wondering when you were going to join me again.'

I put a hand to my aching skull and, while I don't feel any blood, my skin is tender to touch and I must have bruised badly, either externally or internally.

'How long was I out?' I ask tentatively.

'About half an hour,' Parker replies as he continues to stand very casually in front of where I sit before him on a kitchen chair. 'The real question is, how long were you outside my house spying on me?'

That is not a question that I want to answer if I can help it, but I might not have a choice. It's not as if Parker doesn't have the upper hand here, plus maybe it's better if I try and keep him happy so this doesn't get any worse for me.

'Not long,' I say. 'Ten minutes, maybe.'

'Not long,' Parker repeats with a chuckle. 'You think what you were doing was okay because you were only out there for ten minutes. Spying on me for an hour, now that would be bad, but ten minutes? That's perfectly fine, don't worry about it. No harm done. Off you go.'

I might be concussed, but I'm not too far gone to realise that Parker is being sarcastic with me.

'Okay, so the next question is, why were you spying on me?' Parker asks. 'What made you follow me here? I presume that's what you did. Then what made you sneak around to the back of my house and peep through all the windows? You must have a good reason, and I'm dying to hear it.'

I do have a good reason. A very good one. It's because I was warned about this man and what might be hidden here. But how can I say that? And how can I say that the warning came from his father?

Like an accused person in court with very little defence, silence might be my best strategy, so I decide to stay quiet and see what Parker chooses to do next. But like an expert lawyer for the prosecution, he has plenty of tricks up his sleeve to get what he wants, and refusing to say anything is not going to throw him off his stride.

'I'm guessing I either said something to make you not trust me, or somebody else said something,' he goes on, pacing now, as if that's helping his thoughts come quicker. 'While you were unconscious, I've been thinking about what I might have said that could have made you suspicious of me, but I haven't been able to come up with anything. That must mean it was something that somebody else said. So who could that be? Who else knows me well enough to say something to you about me? I'm guessing it was my dear old dad, right?'

He's already figured it out, so there's no need for me to answer, but I have thought of something worthwhile to say.

'Please. Just let me go,' I say quietly. 'I shouldn't have come here, but I haven't seen anything and, if you let me go, I'll just leave. I won't bother you again.'

Will that work? It's a very simple plan, but sometimes they can be the most effective. Sadly not in this case, if the grin on Parker's face is anything to go by.

'I was trying to help you,' he says with a shake of the head. 'I took pity on you. I could see you needed money, but not just money. You needed purpose. I tried to give you that. I had you looking after my father. I thought I could trust you. I thought you'd be able to ignore whatever he told you about me and just put it down to his condition. But I guess not. I guess I should have picked somebody else.'

As I stare at this deceptive, possibly deadly man, I cannot believe I was once attracted to him. How could I miss what was staring me right in the face all along? He's dangerous, and I totally missed it until it was too late.

'I don't know what is going on here, but you don't have to hurt me,' I say. 'Please. You're right, your dad was talking nonsense. I should have just ignored him. I obviously wish I had done now. But I didn't. I guess I'm gullible. But just let me go and you'll never see me again, I swear.'

I came here because I was worried that Parker might be dangerous. But now that he has caught me, I cannot even begin to imagine the danger I could be in.

He's actually right.

I really shouldn't have listened to his dad.

But it's far too late for that.

Parker continues pacing and, the more I watch him, the more I get the sense that he is still making his mind up as to what to do to me. That gives me some hope, possibly false hope, but it's all I have to cling on to, so I'll take it.

'I know you are a good man. You're right. You were helping me by giving me a job, and I'm grateful for that. I needed the money, and I enjoyed working for you. You also helped me when I fell over outside. You've brought me in here and made sure I'm okay, even though I was trespassing on your land. So, again, thank you. You've been too kind to me. I don't deserve it.'

I might be laying it on a little thick, but it's worth a shot to play dumb and make out like I'm a damsel in distress who is more grateful to my captor than afraid of him. But is he going to fall for it and let me go?

'You've been lying to me,' Parker says, suddenly stopping. 'You're not helping me at all. You're investigating me.'

'Investigating? No, I'm not. I'm here by myself.'

'But you're still investigating me. What is it you're expecting to find? What is it my father has told you about me?'

'Nothing.'

'There you go, lying again!' Parker snaps back, and that's the first time he's raised his voice with me, so this is getting worse, not better.

'Well, you've been lying to me too,' I say, taking a risk, but it is the truth.

'What?'

'You've lied. You told me you couldn't afford professional care for Joe, yet look at this house you live in. You're rich! So why did you pretend like you had less money than you do?'

Parker pauses now, clearly not having expected me to turn this back on him, but I'm only being honest. If I'm a liar, so is he.

'It's none of your business,' he says eventually. 'What I choose to tell you and what I choose to keep undisclosed is for me to decide.'

'It's just strange,' I forge on. 'I don't understand the need for lies. Why not just put your dad in a nice home? Why go to the trouble of hiring me?'

'Can't you see? I can't have my father in a home because I can't trust what he might say to somebody. He's obviously told you some things, hasn't he?'

So that's it. He *can* afford a nursing home, but he deliberately chose a cheaper option, which was me, because he was worried his father might say something that could get him in trouble. He obviously didn't think I was a threat. He must have thought I wouldn't listen to Joe, or care about what I heard, and that I'd be happy to keep taking the cash. But I wasn't. I needed to know the truth, so I came here, and now look what's happened.

'Can I leave?' I ask again, trying my luck, but Parker lets out a deep sigh.

'No. You've seen too much.'

'I haven't seen anything!' I try.

'Oh really. You didn't see me making food and taking it into that room?' Parker asks, pointing to the closed door I watched him enter while I was peeping through the window earlier.

'No,' I say, shaking my head to reinforce my lie.

'It doesn't matter if you did,' Parker says with a shrug, which unsettles me. 'So what if you know things about me that you shouldn't. I guess that makes us equal.'

'What do you mean equal?'

'I know some things about you that I'm guessing I shouldn't,' Parker goes on. 'Quite interesting things actually.'

What the hell is he talking about?

'Do you want to know what I know and how I know it?' he asks me, and I have a feeling he's going to tell me whatever I say, so I stay quiet and watch him as he walks over to a drawer and pulls it open. Then he takes something out and, when I see what it is, I gasp.

It's my notebook.

He must have been the one who took it from my apartment.

That means I'm not the only one to have been trespassing on private property.

Parker visited my home long before I visited his.

But why?

TWENTY-EIGHT

"'Dear Darcy,'" Parker starts to read from my diary, "'You need to read this every single day and do as I say. We are your family, and we love you, but we cannot be with you. You're safer away from here and you will be safe as long as you stay away. Look at our photos every day and make sure you remember us like we will remember you. But make sure you do as I say on the next page. It's crucial that you do. Love you sis, Pippa.'" Parker finishes reading the words on that particular page of my diary and, having already read out the names of my family members on the previous page, he turns to the last one and reads what is written there: "'Never watch the news. Never ever come back home.'"

If those warnings were unsettling to read, they're even more unsettling to hear read out to me by a man who won't let me leave his house. At least I presume I can't leave. The only way to truly test it would be to run for the kitchen door, but I'm guessing it's either locked or he'll catch me before I get there. I'd rather not test it, at least not yet, because if it goes wrong, I'll know for sure that I'm stuck here. At least by holding off on running, I maintain a glimmer of hope of getting out of this.

'That's a very interesting letter that this person called Pippa wrote you,' Parker says as he looks down at the notebook again. 'And those are two very interesting warnings. Never watch the news. Never ever come back home. My, I wonder why she has to tell you to do such dramatic things? I'd love to know. Care to enlighten me?'

Parker looks very intrigued and waits for me to answer, but all I can think about is why he would break into my apartment while I was out and steal that notebook he's just been reciting from. For me to get here, I had to follow him home, so for him to have that, he must have followed me home first.

'Why?' I ask, answering a question with a more urgent one of my own. 'Why did you steal that?'

'You think I'd just hire a total stranger to look after my father?' Parker replies with a laugh. 'I wanted to do a little research.'

'By breaking into my home and stealing my personal property?'

'It's just a notebook.'

'You had no right to take it! And you had no right to be in my apartment when I wasn't there.'

'Just like you had no right to be creeping around outside my house tonight?'

I realise this is pointless – we've both done a similar thing, so Parker is always going to say that I am in the wrong and I'd say vice versa. We're stuck, except there is one difference. I still don't know who Parker really is, though thanks to that notebook in his hand, he knows more about me.

'Okay, you've got me. I have been lying to you, and I am hiding something,' he admits. 'But I'm obviously not the only one, and now I really want to know – what is it that you're hiding, Darcy? It sure sounds good, and it must even be news-worthy if Pippa thinks you should avoid watching the news. You can never go home either? Wow, what have you done?'

The truth is that I don't know what it is that I have done in my past, because I can't remember. But I doubt Parker would believe me if I was to tell him that, so what else can I say to improve my situation?

'Let's assume we've both done things we shouldn't have,' I say, looking Parker in the eyes. 'That would mean we both have a strong reason why we wouldn't want the police to get involved with either of us. I don't want them prying and neither do you. So, in that case, the best thing for both of us would be that we go our separate ways. That way, neither of us gets into trouble. That sound fair?'

I really hope it does – it's about all I've got.

Parker thinks about what I've said for a moment before he takes another look at my notebook.

'There's an address here,' he says. 'A house in Chicago. Is that where your family live?'

'What does that matter?'

'I'm just curious,' he says. 'The address, and the way this Pippa person, who is apparently your sister, has written to you with specific instructions. It's as if she is talking to somebody who doesn't know who they are. Is that the case, Darcy? Do you not know who you really are?'

Parker has landed on my truth – the fact that my past is almost as mysterious to me as it is to him – and suddenly I see a better way out of this.

'I have problems with my memory,' I confess, though I'm not just saying this to be truthful but because it might increase my chances of him allowing me to leave.

'What kind of problems?' Parker asks, looking up from the notebook and sounding intrigued.

'I forget things.'

'What things?'

'Anything that happened more than a few weeks ago. I can't remember any of it.'

Parker ponders that for a moment.

'You don't remember anything?'

I shake my head.

'How is that possible? Is it amnesia?'

'I guess so. I don't really know. I can't remember what caused it, obviously. And by the sounds of what Pippa wrote for me, I don't want to know.'

Parker seems very interested now, but I'm only interested in one thing.

'So, if you let me go, I won't remember any of this in a few weeks,' I explain. 'I won't remember you or your dad or whatever else is going on here. So you've got nothing to worry about. You can let me just walk out the door.'

Parker is still quiet, so I hope that means he's thinking about it. While he's doing that, I have already decided that, once I'm clear of here, I will pack up my things and leave, and once I'm somewhere he can't ever find me again, I'll make an anonymous call to the police telling them to come here and check this house. More specifically, check what's in his basement. That way, if there is something wrong here, I can still put a stop to it and give help to anybody who might need it.

'Nice try,' Parker says, slamming my notebook shut before laughing to himself. 'But you're not getting out of here whatever you try and tell me, so you might as well stop wasting your time.'

It didn't work, and now I'm out of options.

Well, almost.

I spring up off the chair and run to the kitchen door before twisting the handle and praying that it opens. But it's locked, just like I feared it might be, and just as Parker clearly made sure it was.

'Unlucky,' he says behind me, but I'm not giving up yet, so I try and run past him to get to another door in the house. But he grabs me and, despite my wriggling and trying to kick him, he doesn't let me go.

'I told you, Darcy, you're not going anywhere,' he says before he pushes me back in the direction of the chair I just left so abruptly. But there's no way I'm sitting down again. The time for calm conversation is over. If I know I can't get out of here, what have I got to lose?

I pick up the chair and, before Parker can fully get his hands up to shield himself, I throw it at him. As it hits him, he cries out in pain. But I don't hang around to see how bad his injuries are. All I do is rush past him on my way to the front door.

I reach it in seconds and try the handle again, but it's locked too. I won't give up so easily this time. Once I spot the window nearby, I start looking for something I can use to break the glass. I'll climb over broken shards if I have to, and when I see the coat stand, I pick it up and prepare to plunge it through the window. But the stand is suddenly snatched from my hands before a hand goes over my mouth and I'm dragged back towards the kitchen.

I try to scream or cry out for help or even just bite the palm and fingers that are covering my mouth, but I can't do any of it, and then I get pushed down to the floor. Parker is standing over me again, like he was outside when I banged my head, only this time I'm not about to lose consciousness. Maybe it would be better if I did, but unfortunately I'm very much awake, which is why I get to hear what Parker has to say next.

'There's only one door down here that isn't locked right now,' he tells me as I gasp for breath. 'It's the door over there, just behind you. You know the one, right?'

I turn around and see the door he's talking about. It's the same door I saw him taking the food into earlier before he caught me.

'You're so desperate to find out what's inside,' Parker goes on, seemingly enjoying this moment. 'Then why not take a look? Go on. Be my guest. Open that door, and then you'll know what my father was really talking about.'

TWENTY-NINE

PIPPA

How do you save a marriage? Tell the truth, possibly.

How do you destroy a marriage? Admit to homicide and hiding two bodies, definitely.

I stare at my husband and wait to see what he has to say about everything I've just told him. The reason it's taking a while for him to respond is because I've told him a lot.

I've told him everything.

Laurence. Eden. Darcy. My parents. Lake Michigan. How long the prison sentences are likely to be for my crimes and, most importantly, how long I'd be away from our family if I was to get caught. Life, most probably, with no possibility of parole.

That's why I can't blame him for not responding to me yet.

But while his lack of words isn't telling me what he's thinking or feeling, his body is doing a good job of it. He looks stiff, tense, his shoulders raised and his hands clasped together. His face is twisted in disbelief, and I can see his breathing is laboured. But it's his eyes that are the biggest giveaway, at least in terms of how he is feeling about me.

That's because they aren't looking at me.

They're looking at everything else but me.

'You wanted the truth,' I remind him, which might not be helpful, but I have to say something to break this awful silence. 'So there it is. That's the truth. Now you know why I've been hiding things from you. Now you know why I've been so distant. I was trying to protect you. I was protecting both you and our son.'

I can't be any more honest than that, but something in my last statement has riled Karl up because he suddenly puts his gaze on me.

'You think this is protecting us?' he asks in a chilling tone of voice I've never heard him use before. 'You think doing all these awful things is protecting me and Campbell? Are you crazy? You've put us in danger too!'

'No, you're not in any danger!'

'Aren't we? How can you be so sure?'

'Because it's under control!'

'The police have found the body of the woman you killed! That doesn't seem very under control to me! And you killed her to keep your sister's secrets. So you're protecting her, but what have we got to do with this? What have Campbell or I done to deserve getting wrapped up in any of this?'

'Karl, please. Just let me explain.'

'No, you've already explained, and I wish you hadn't, because you've really put me in an awful situation now.'

'What do you mean?'

'You've told me about two serious crimes. Just because a conversation between husband and wife can't be used in court doesn't mean it's no big deal. I'll still be in a very uncomfortable position if I do get questioned about this by the police. I'd rather have never known! Now I feel as guilty as you, and Darcy, and your goddamn parents!'

'No, it's not like that. You shouldn't feel guilty. You've done nothing wrong.'

'I know that, but now you've told me, what am I supposed to

do if I get questioned about this information? Lie? Or just say no comment, which will only make you seem even guiltier!'

The volume of our heated discussion is loud enough to bring our son back into the room, Campbell appearing in the doorway looking very worried – he's heard his parents raising their voices at each other. We should be grateful that he's too young to truly understand the gravity of what we're saying, although we're not grateful for the fact that we're upsetting him by being like this.

'I'm sorry for shouting,' I say as I rush to my son and try to comfort him, but he pulls away from me and goes to his father instead, stinging me, although it's not the first time a child has chosen one parent over the other after a disagreement. But this feels more symbolic. As I stand on one side of the room while I look at my husband and son on the other, I feel there is a chasm between us that I cannot bridge again.

We're separating, and if I can't get them back, freedom won't be the worst thing I lose.

It'll be them.

There's also the issue that if Karl and I are no longer husband and wife, he could testify against me in court. Would it ever come to that? If it did, the information I've given him could ruin me. I ultimately told Karl everything because I thought our history together would mean he would be loyal and protect me. But have I been incredibly naïve?

I don't remember there being anything in our marriage vows about keeping secrets from the police.

'I think you need to go,' Karl says as Campbell snuggles into him, making me wish my boy was being like that with me.

'Go? Go where?'

'I don't know. Anywhere. Your parents' place. I just don't think you should be here right now.'

Karl looks like he means it, but I'm not leaving them. The only way that is going to happen is if a police officer drags me

174   DANIEL HURST

kicking and screaming from this house and, until that happens,
I'm not giving up.

'Please, don't do this. There's still a way. There's still a
chance this doesn't have to be the end.'

'Really?' Karl asks, and he grabs the remote control and
turns the TV back on. Instantly, the screen is filled with
images of police officers and forensic experts standing beside
Lake Michigan, and my husband points at the screen for
emphasis.

'Look at this! Tell me there's a chance everything is going to
be okay now?'

I don't need to look at the screen to know that it's bad, but
Campbell doesn't understand the severity of what he's seeing so
he innocently calls out 'police' before sitting down and
watching the TV. After experiencing several days over these
few short years where I've wished he was a little older so things
would be easier with him, I'm so glad now that he is the age he
is because he's still so innocent. So naïve. So oblivious to adult
life and adult problems.

But there is an adult standing beside him, and he knows
how bad this is.

But he must also know how he could make this better.

'Come here,' I say, gesturing for Karl to follow me out of the
room and, while he hesitates, I walk away until he has no choice
but to follow. He must know that I have something to say to him
that is best said out of earshot of our son, and I do. Only when
he has joined me in the hallway do I speak again.

'Look at that,' I say, pointing to a photo on the wall that
shows the three of us by a pool in Hawaii. 'Remember that day?
How hot it was? How badly we slept because Campbell was
jetlagged. We all were. But look at us. We were so happy.
Because we were together, and we knew how lucky we were.
No matter the tiredness or the hard work and expense of getting
there, we knew that we were blessed to be a family.'

'What are you doing?' Karl asks me, but I move his attention on to the next photo.

'Look at this one. You remember when this was taken, right? A week after we'd brought Campbell home from the hospital. You can see how tired we both are, but it's our first proper family photo together.'

Karl stares at the image of me and him, looking weary as we hold our sleeping newborn in our arms.

'Stop it,' he says, but I'm not done yet.

'Campbell's first day at kindergarten,' I say, moving on to another photo. 'And here's us on our honeymoon. And here we are in New York for our anniversary.'

'Pippa, stop it,' Karl tries again, but I haven't finished making my point.

'All these memories. All these happy times. But they don't have to end. We can make more. But we can only do that if we stick together as a family.'

'Are you crazy? Those photos were taken before I found out you were a killer,' Karl says aggressively under his breath.

'I only did it because I was saving my family and trying to defend myself!' I insist. 'Would you not do the same for us? Would you not kill for me, or our son, if you had no other choice?'

That question stops Karl from being so confident with his answers, and I make sure to reinforce my point while it's still landing with him.

'There's a big difference between what I have done and what another criminal might have done,' I say. 'Some people break the law and hurt people for pleasure or for their own gain. I did it because it was the only way to keep the people I love most safe. You. Campbell. My sister. My parents. Everything I do and everything I do from this point on will be and has always been for all of you. If that makes me a bad person and someone you want to leave, I don't know what else I can do.'

Karl thinks about that – he isn't telling me to leave yet, nor is he getting our son and leaving himself, so maybe there's a chance.

'Is there any way the police can trace this back to you or your family?' he asks me after a moment.

'I don't think so,' is my best reply. 'We'll just have to hope for the best.'

That answer must hardly fill my husband with confidence, but he's still thinking about it, and I take his hand to give him even more to consider.

'I hate what has happened to us recently, but this doesn't have to be the end. Our family can be saved. *We* can still be saved. I love you. I know that more than ever right now. So let's fight. Trust me, there is a chance this might all go away.'

It sounds ridiculous to say it when our son is watching a news report about the discovery of the body his mother and grandfather put in the lake, but if I can't be optimistic then the only other alternative is to cry. Mercifully, Karl doesn't let go of my hand. In fact, he gives it a gentle squeeze.

'Okay,' he says quietly.

'Okay you'll keep this quiet?' I ask, needing confirmation, and Karl takes a few seconds to reply before nodding.

Do I believe him? I have no choice but to. Surely he wouldn't lie to me, not when he knows what's at stake here.

Maybe I am right. Maybe everything can be okay. But that blissful moment of sheer ignorance is shattered a few seconds later when my phone rings and I see that it's Dad calling me.

'Yes, I know we need to talk,' I say after answering the call. 'Shall I come over to you or do you guys want to come here?'

'Pippa, shut up! It's too late for that! They're here!'

Dad's panicked voice sends a chill through my entire body, and Karl looks frozen too when he sees my shock.

'What are you talking about? Who's there?'

'The police! They're outside our house now! They're coming to the door!'

'What is it?' Karl asks me, unable to hear the other end of the line. But that's a good thing. If he knew what was happening at my mom and dad's place now, he'd surely start panicking. He'd probably take Campbell and leave as quickly as he could.

He'd do that because, if the police are already there, surely it's only a matter of time until they turn up here...

THIRTY

DARCY

I don't know what Parker thinks is going to happen, but there is no way I'm going to open that door and enter his basement. If I do that, I'll be even more trapped than I am at the moment. At least out here in the main house I have a chance. If only I can get away from him again, and have a few more seconds, I could break that window and I could get out of here. But my captor is still standing over me and, suddenly, because I haven't moved, he decides to move me.

'Fine, I'll show you what's in there myself,' he says impatiently as he pulls me to my feet. I do my best to be a dead weight and make myself harder for him to move, but he still drags me towards the basement door.

'No! Get off me!' I cry, but it's useless. As we reach the door, Parker risks taking one hand off me to pull the handle. I try to use that moment to wriggle free, but he quickly returns that hand to my waist, holding me tightly and pushing me forward into what is now an open doorway.

I want to shoot out my own hands and grab the doorframe – that would enable me to offer some resistance – but Parker has such a strong grip of me, and my arms are forced down uselessly by my side rather than outwards in a more helpful position.

We pass through the doorway and the light in the kitchen fades as we enter a dark space. But as scary as this is, I'm almost glad I can't see anything in here, at least not yet anyway. Seeing something might be worse than seeing nothing at all.

'Mind the step,' Parker says, but before I can even ask him what step he is referring to, I feel myself going down and just about manage to keep my footing as we move onto what must be a staircase.

It's extremely unnerving to be moving down a flight of steps when you can't even see your feet, almost as unnerving as being manhandled by a dangerous aggressor, but we're still moving down and, anytime I almost fall, Parker increases his grip on me to keep me upright. But he's not being a gentleman. He's merely holding on to me to stop me escaping, and the further down we go, the less chance there is of that.

I stumble again but not because there are more steps. It's because they've suddenly stopped and we're back on flat ground again. As usual, Parker keeps me from losing my balance. I look back the way we came and see a tiny glimmer of light from the kitchen that we just left.

How I wish we were still up there now. It seemed bad at the time, but I'd give anything to trade this dark basement. Though the basement isn't dark for long. I hear a switch being flicked before the space is flooded with light. I have to squint my eyes to help them adjust to the drastic change.

'You wanted to see what was going on here,' Parker says, slowly letting go of me. 'So take a look.'

I blink a couple more times until my eyesight adjusts and, when it does, I really wish I hadn't come here tonight. That's because I see that Parker and I aren't the only ones down here. There's somebody else too. A woman.

Or at least I think she's a woman.

It's hard to tell – whoever it is, in the corner of this basement, is sitting slumped on the floor with their back to us and long, dark, scraggly hair covering their face. I note the empty plate on the ground nearby, the same plate I saw Parker carry in here earlier. This must be who the food was for. This poor person, whoever they are. What kind of place is this for them to eat a meal? And what kind of condition are they in? They don't look well at all. They haven't even turned around to look at us yet.

Are they too ill?

Or too afraid?

'What do you think?' Parker asks me now. 'Wish you'd stayed at home instead of following me back here?'

The answer to that is obvious, but what is not obvious is who this person is. I'm about to ask if she's okay when Parker speaks again.

'Let me introduce you two to each other. Darcy, this is Irene.'

Irene? His girlfriend? The one Joe mentioned?

It's clear now what that man was trying to warn me about. This is the woman I was supposed to help. So Joe knows about this? How long has it been going on?

Irene still hasn't turned around to look at us, but Parker doesn't seem bothered about that. He just pushes me forward towards her and I fall to the floor, landing next to her. I see her flinch as I come close.

'What are you doing? You can't get away with this! Let us both go!' I cry as I look back at Parker, but horrifyingly he is walking back up the stairs.

'I'll leave the light on for you,' he says as he goes, as if that is doing us a favour. 'That way you will be able to see each other's faces while you talk. I imagine you have lots of questions to ask each other.'

'No, wait!' I cry, getting up off the ground and trying to

catch up with Parker before he can close the door. But I hear a weak, frightened voice behind me.

'Don't bother,' it says, and I turn around to look at Irene, who has now lifted her head to acknowledge me. 'He's always quicker and he'll only take more pleasure if you bang on the door after he's locked it.'

Irene must be speaking from experience, a grim, awful experience, but one she has endured nevertheless. The delay she's caused means Parker has reached the top of the stairs and the door is starting to close behind him.

I want to run towards it. I want to try and stop Parker from trapping me in here. But something about the way Irene looks and speaks tells me she's right.

It's pointless.

He'll win.

So I stay where I am, down in the basement with the malnourished, sleep-deprived prisoner.

Then we both hear the sound of the key turning in the lock.

THIRTY-ONE

PIPPA

'What the hell am I going to say?' Dad asks me, his anxious voice coming down the line, allowing his nervousness to seep into my home too, even though there's currently several miles between us.

'Just stay calm,' I reply, but that might be the most ridiculous thing a person has ever said, especially in these circumstances. Dad is freaking out because the police are parking outside his house, the same house where Eden was murdered, and where her body was put into my father's car and driven to the lake. Now that lake is all over the news and the body has been found and, somehow, the police are already on the right track with their investigation.

I have no idea how or why they knew to go to my mom and dad's place so soon after the discovery of the body.

Bu they're there now.

And in a second, Dad will have to open the door to them.

'I have to go,' he says, and I guess he's about to hang up.

'No, wait! Stay on the line!' I cry before he cuts me off and I'm left in a silence that will be drowned in worry.

'What?'

'Don't disconnect this call. Keep it open. Put your phone down somewhere so I can hear what the police are saying,' I instruct my father urgently.

'I can't.'

'Yes, you can. Just do it, Dad. I need to hear what's going on! I need to hear how much the police know!'

I hear knocking in the background. The police are at his door. Dad has to go and answer it now. He does as I ask and keeps the call open.

'What the hell is going on?' Karl asks me, but I put a finger to my lips to tell him to shut up before pressing my phone even closer to my ear.

I hear some muffled voices and fear I'm not going to be able to hear everything that is said, but then the voices come closer and I guess the police are entering the home.

'Is it just you in the house, sir?' a gruff male voice asks.

'No, my wife is here too,' Dad answers.

'Okay, go and get her, please,' comes the stern instruction, and I hear Dad calling out for Mom, who is most likely hiding away upstairs somewhere with a glass of wine and trying not to have a panic attack. I hope she's successful, or it's going to be a big giveaway when she comes down the stairs hyperventilating.

As I wait for my parents to return to the area where the phone is, I hear another male voice.

'Nice house,' he says, and I guess the detective or police officer, whoever it is, is impressed with where my parents live. They should be, it's an amazing property, but my family really do not want to be getting any kind of attention from the police.

'What's going on?' I hear Dad ask, and he must be back.

'My name is Detective Burgoyne and I need you both to answer a few questions,' the first male voice says, and my heart skips a beat. Mom and Dad must be feeling even worse – they're the ones who are going to have to answer those questions.

'Questions about what?' Mom chirps, and it's a pleasant surprise to hear that her voice sounds strong. Maybe she is holding it together better than I thought she would.

'We are trying to locate your daughter,' is what I hear next, and I almost drop my phone.

Oh my god. The police are looking for me. This is it. It's over.

'Pippa, what is it?' my husband asks me, but I ignore him and keep listening to events at the other end of the line.

'I have two daughters,' Dad tells the detective.

'We're looking for Darcy,' comes the response. I can breathe a sigh of relief for all of two seconds before I realise this is still bad news. Of course they're looking for my sister. If they were looking for me then they'd be here already. But if they want Darcy, that must mean they are onto something, and now I'm really glad I got her to leave the city before this happened.

'Why are you looking for Darcy?' Mom asks.

'We have a few questions for her,' comes the surly reply.

'She's not here and we don't know where she is,' Dad tells the detective and however many investigating officers are surrounding him.

'You don't know where your own daughter is?' Burgoyne asks.

'That's right. We have no idea,' Mom adds.

'I find that hard to believe,' the moody male says, and I fear this is not going well. But then Mom takes over.

'You wouldn't if you knew what had been happening with my daughter over these last few years,' she says, still speaking in a clear and controlled fashion, which is very impressive in the circumstances. 'She was in an accident, and she's lost her memory. She doesn't know who we are unless we constantly remind her and, worse, she doesn't even know herself. We've been through hell as a family and then, one day, we woke up to find that Darcy had left. She hasn't told us where she is. So to answer your question, detective, that is why we don't know where our daughter is, and the sad truth is we might never see her again.'

A silence descends and I worry for a second that the call has somehow disconnected, but then I hear a voice again.

'I'm sorry,' it says. It's the detective, or rather the sheepish detective now that Mom has just shot him down.

'Why do you need to talk to her?' Dad asks. That is the most pertinent question, and I hold my breath, as I imagine my parents are doing too, as we wait for the answer.

'It's in connection with the body of the woman found in Lake Michigan earlier today,' Detective Burgoyne replies.

'What's that got to do with Darcy?' Mom cries.

'I believe that the deceased was a former friend and colleague of hers,' the detective goes on. 'Her name is Eden Carthy. Does that ring any bells?'

It's ringing all sorts of bells, but not any the detective can know about. I pray that my parents are still keeping their emotions in check. I'm losing my mind here but I'm not the one in front of a detective and several officers, although I might be very soon if this gets worse.

'Oh my goodness, Eden is dead?'

That attempt at acting shocked was made by my mother, and while it's hard to know exactly how it went down in the room, it actually sounded convincing via the phone.

'I'm afraid so,' the detective replies. 'You knew the deceased well?'

'Not well, exactly, but we knew of her,' Mom goes on. 'We knew she worked with our daughter, but that was a long time ago. You say she's dead? That's awful, what happened?' Mom is acting as though she's up for an Oscar. The detective says he is not at liberty to disclose any more details at this stage.

'I don't understand. What does this have to do with Darcy?' Dad asks.

'We've been informed that your daughter was trying to locate Eden three months ago, which is around the time she went missing.'

I quickly think about who could have told the police about that and then I remember the nurses' reunion I accompanied my sister to, back when she was trying to get some answers about all the flashbacks she was having. We spoke to a nurse there and Eden was discussed. What was that nurse's name again? Cara, was it? She must have been the one to mention to the police that she knew the deceased when the news came through today, as well as knew someone who had been searching for her before she vanished.

Cara probably thought she was being helpful by passing on Darcy's name and, as far as the police are concerned, she was.

But she's been very unhelpful to my family.

'Wait a minute. You think Darcy has something to do with Eden's death?' Dad cries. 'No, absolutely not! That's preposterous!'

'Like I said, we would just like to ask her a few questions,' the detective tries again.

'And like we said, we have no idea where she is, so you can't,' Mom snaps back.

'When did your daughter leave?' the detective asks, and that is a very clever question. He's clearly trying to ascertain if Darcy's disappearance coincided with Eden's.

'Erm,' I hear Dad stall, and that's not good. Mom isn't speaking either.

Somebody please say something, and quick.

'Not that long ago, was it?' Dad answers eventually. 'Maybe a month or two?'

Oh god, he's lying to the police.

'Yeah, just over a month ago,' Mom says, and now she's lying too.

The truth is Darcy left Chicago just after Eden, and indeed

Laurence, vanished, which was three months ago. But if the detective knew that then it would only pour gasoline onto his burning suspicions.

'You're sure about that?' the detective asks, and neither of my parents say anything in disagreement, so I guess that's their version of events and now they have to stick to it. That also means I'll have to stick to it if the police ask me any questions, but fingers crossed, this is the only time they'll bother us. Then Mom goes and says something daring.

'Do you know that Eden was dating Laurence before they both disappeared?' she asks, and the detective confirms that he was aware of that. 'Well then, don't you think it's obvious what has happened? Laurence must have hurt Eden and hid her body in the lake before going on the run. That's why they both went missing at the same time. It makes perfect sense.'

Mom might think it does, and we might all wish the detective thought it did too.

'Early examination of Eden's body reveals that she died very recently,' the detective informs my parents. 'Not three months ago, when they were both reported missing, but within the last thirty-six hours or so. Therefore, her time of death does not correspond with their disappearance. That means we cannot simply assume Laurence is a suspect.'

That's not great to hear.

'We are, however, stepping up our efforts to locate Laurence, and should we find him, dead or alive, that will change things drastically. But until then, we are going to be looking for your daughter. If she gets in touch, please let her know that she is to contact us as soon as possible.'

It sounds like the conversation, or interrogation, is coming to a close, but I can't breathe a sigh of relief. Not after what I just heard.

The police are stepping up their efforts to find Laurence.

Dead or alive.

Oh no. What if they are wondering if his body might be near to where Eden's was found?

What if they're searching in that area of the lake now?

What if they find him, so they know he's not a suspect anymore?

That would just leave Darcy.

'One more thing,' the detective says. 'I'm going to go and speak to your other daughter. Pippa, is it? We've been informed that she was with Darcy while she was trying to locate Eden three months ago. We have an address here for her. Can you confirm that it's correct?'

My world stands still as I listen to the detective reading out my correct home address to my parents, both of whom have no choice but to confirm that it's right and that's where the police can find me. Then I hear the detective say his goodbyes, and there's the sound of several people walking away before I hear a door close and, a minute later, my dad is back on the phone.

'Did you hear that?' he asks me, and I confirm that I did.

'So you know what's happening then,' Dad goes on. 'The police are on their way. They want to speak to you next.'

THIRTY-TWO

DARCY

This all started because I was supposed to be helping Parker's dad, Joe. Now I'm trapped in a room with someone who needs my help more. It's Parker's girlfriend, Irene – or, as I'm presuming now, his ex-girlfriend.

'How long have you been down here?' I ask Irene less than a minute after our captor has left us alone together, locking the basement door but at least leaving the light on so we could see each other.

'I don't know. I've lost track of time,' comes the grim answer. 'What's the date?'

That should be an easy question for someone who has been living in the outside world to answer, but I have to think about it for an extra second, another symptom of my brain not operating at full capacity. When I give Irene the date, she looks even sadder than she did when I first saw her.

'It's been a month then,' she says solemnly, her face still mostly covered by her greasy, unkept hair, but I catch a few glimpses of her eyes and it's as if the light went off in there a while ago.

'A month! Oh my god, you've been down here all this time?'

Irene doesn't need to confirm that though. Sadly, her appearance tells me it's true.

'Why? Why is he doing this to you?' is my next question.

'Because he's crazy,' Irene replies. 'He's evil. He's a monster.'

All of that is obvious, at least at this point, but surely there has to be more to it than that.

'You were his girlfriend, right?' I ask, and Irene nods, though only after several long seconds in which it looked like even that simple gesture would be a challenge for her. She really needs to get out of here and get some medical attention. Not only that, but looking at her is offering me a glimpse into what I'll look like if I don't get out of here too, not that I need any more motivation on that front.

'So what happened? Did you guys have a fight? There must be some reason why he locked you down here.'

'There is,' Irene says, her voice raspy, but there's no water down here to soothe her throat. 'But it's not worthy of this.'

'What is it?'

'I cheated on him.'

That's a surprise, but unfortunately infidelity happens all the time. I've never known it result in the guilty party being locked in a basement and, by the looks of it, practically left to die.

'That's it? He locked you in here because you had an affair?'

'It wasn't even an affair! I was drunk at a bar one night and kissed some random guy, but he saw me, although I didn't know at the time. I felt bad about it and, the next day, he messaged, asking me to come over. I figured I'd keep my secret and everything would be fine, but he was tricking me. Once I was here, he said he had something to show me down here. Then he locked me in.'

It's such a simple story, but it's totally insane that Parker

would think to even do something like this, never mind expect
to get away with it.

'He only told me that he'd seen me with that guy when I
begged him to let me know what he was doing,' Irene goes on,
tears running down her pale, gaunt face. 'He said I'd hurt him,
and this was my punishment. I told him I was sorry and begged
him to let me go, but he never listens. He just brings me tiny
amounts of food and water, I guess enough to keep me alive, but
that's it.'

It's awful. All of it. Just terrible. And now I'm caught up in
the middle.

'I guess you're his new girlfriend,' Irene says, sobbing even
more now. 'All I can think is what happened to the one before
me? She must be dead, right? Now, I'm next. Then it'll be you.
Then somebody else. How long has he been getting away with
this?'

Irene is really working herself up into a terrible state, and
any hopes I might have had that my presence here might offer
her some small slivers of encouragement are extinguished.
Being in here with her is making her feel worse. She thinks
Parker must do this to different women all the time.

But perhaps not.

'I'm not his girlfriend,' I tell her. 'I was working for him. I
was helping care for his dad.'

'Joe?' Irene asks, and I nod.

'Parker said he couldn't afford a nursing home for his father,
so he's been paying me to look after him.'

'He said he can't afford a nursing home? The guy's loaded!'

'I know that now,' I say quietly, only too aware of how easily
Parker duped me.

'But if you were looking after Joe, what are you doing here?'
Irene asks next.

'Joe said some things that were concerning me,' I explain.

'He was making out like his son had something to hide. Then he mentioned you.'

'Me?'

'Yes. Is it possible he knew you were trapped down here?'

Irene thinks about it, but then shakes her head.

'No, Joe is nice! He would have called the police if he knew what Parker was doing!'

Irene might think that, because that's what a normal, rational person would do. But Joe is conflicted.

'It's his son,' I remind her. 'I'm not sure how easy it is for a father to report their son for a crime, but I'm guessing it's not simple.'

'So what? He was just dropping hints to you?' Irene asks.

'I guess so. That must mean he had some idea that something was wrong here. He must have realised something was going on, but has been too scared to do anything about it himself, so he told me to take a look.'

'The coward! Now you're stuck too! Maybe it was a trap!'

Irene's suggestion is a startling one. Did Joe trick me into following his son home because he knew I'd get caught and end up in this basement too? Are this father and son working together to trap poor women like us and, if so, how long have they been getting away with it? Is Joe even ill at all?

'We don't know what's really going on,' I tell Irene, trying to stay sane – it's all too easy to lose your mind while locked in a windowless room. 'Joe could be perfectly innocent, and you might be the first person Parker has locked in here. You said you cheated on him, so he had a motive to want to hurt you. I'm not saying what he's done is right, because it's obviously not, but it's not as if he just did this randomly. He was angry and upset and this is how he chose to take out his anger.'

I think about what Parker told me about his relationship, the length of it, and how that might have led to Irene getting some hints that he might not be as normal as he seemed.

'Did you ever notice anything unusual about him while you were together?' I ask her. 'Any hints or signs that he could be capable of a thing like this?'

'Of course not! Do you think I would have stayed with him if I had?'

'I'm just trying to see if there's anything that might help us.'

'The only thing that can help us is if that door opens! Otherwise, we're dead!'

'But he's kept you alive, and maybe he plans to continue doing so,' I remind the frightened woman. 'Maybe he's going to let you go one day.'

'But now you're here,' Irene says, pointing out the obvious. 'So what does that do for his plan?'

'I don't know,' I admit, looking up the stairs at the locked door.

'And you say he might have been intending to let me go, but it's been a month now. And how would he know I wouldn't just go straight to the police? He doesn't, so that's why he can't let me go. That's why he's going to keep me locked up in here until I die.'

'Irene, calm down,' I try, but it's no good. I'm talking to a woman who has been living this hell for a lot longer than I have.

'We're going to die in here,' she cries, only making this worse for the pair of us, but it's no surprise she's this way. She's had nothing to give her hope over the past month.

'There must be someone on the outside looking for you,' I suddenly suggest. 'There must be someone who knew you were dating Parker, right? Why haven't people been looking for you? Why hasn't he been questioned about your disappearance?'

I'm hoping Irene could give me a positive answer, one that might mention her parents or at least a network of friends who could be hounding the police every day to try and find her. If so, maybe there is a chance she could be located here, especially with her connection to her captor. Maybe her story is on the news. I would have missed it because I've been avoiding all news, but it could be a top story in this part of Florida and, if so, that might help. But I haven't seen any missing persons posters at the beach. I worry that not as many people are looking for Irene as I'd hoped.

'Nobody is looking for me,' she says meekly.

'Nobody? There must be someone?'

'There isn't. I'm not from here. I'm from California. I left home years ago and I've not spoken to anyone in my family since then. I've just travelled around. Worked in different places. This is the fifth state I've lived in in the past ten years.'

That's not promising. A nomadic existence like that means she could be off the grid for a very long time, and nobody would think it unusual, or even notice at all. If that wasn't bad enough, the same could basically be said of me, though Irene doesn't know that yet, which is why she asks me an optimistic question.

'Will people be looking for you?' she asks me, probably not expecting that my backstory is even more varied than hers.

I wish I could say yes. I wish I could say that I had a family who would miss me if they didn't speak to or see me for more than one day, as well as a large group of friends who I was in regular contact with, and they would know something was wrong if I went quiet. But that's not the case. Far from it. All I know about my life is in that notebook that Parker has, and what little there is in there makes for very grim reading.

'I don't think so,' I say sadly, and Irene looks despondent, or at least even more despondent than she already did.

'He tricked me,' I say as I shake my head and feel shame at my stupidity. 'I thought he was a nice guy. I thought there might be something between us one day. All this time, he was dangerous.'

I don't expect Irene to join in on my pity party, because she's surely already gone through that process a long time ago.

But she does, perhaps because she knows misery loves company.

'He tricked us both,' she says before lowering her head and very much looking like she's giving up on any further discussion. But there is something else we can talk about. Perhaps the only thing worth talking about in here at all.

'We need to make a plan,' I say as I stare at that closed door at the top of the stairs. 'We need to figure out how we're going to get out of here. Because we are. Me and you. Working as a team. We're going to get out. If we don't, we're dead. It's as simple as that.'

THIRTY-THREE

PIPPA

It's one thing wondering if the police are going to come to your door. It's another to know they definitely are and there's nothing you can do about it.

I suppose there is one thing I can do.

I could run.

But I'm not going to do that, for a couple of different reasons. One, it would make me look guilty if I did, and I'd like to make the police work a whole lot harder to figure that out if I can.

Two, I can't just run, can I?

I'm an adult with responsibilities. I have a house, a car, a job, all sorts of outgoing payments attached to my bank account, from important ones like the gas bill all the way down to the silly ones like which platform I stream my music from. But they are just things, and they could all be replaced or even forgotten completely if need be. But it's the things I can't just abandon that make it so much harder to run.

One of those things is the man sitting on the sofa opposite me, the one with the cup of coffee in his hand, which he is sipping as it's getting late but we can't go to bed yet. When he suggested coffee, I wasn't sure it was a good idea. Caffeine makes people jittery, and surely being jittery is the last thing a person needs when the police are on their way. But Karl insisted on pouring himself a cup and, in the end, I accepted one too. We could be awake all night. In fact, I know we will. Even if the police come here soon and everything goes okay, I'm hardly likely to just be able to go to bed afterwards and rest easy. Caffeine, therefore, is the only real weapon I have against the fatigue that is gnawing away at me and, without combating it in some way, that fatigue could be the reason I slip up later and say something I shouldn't to the police.

I take a sip of my own coffee while Karl drinks from his at the same time, but it's not the only thing we are doing in unison. We are also looking at our son, who is sitting on the carpet in between us, playing with some toys, even though it's far past his bedtime and he's not normally up this late unless he's deliberately refusing to sleep. There are a few reasons he's not in bed, and Karl and I talked through them all shortly after my call with Dad ended and I knew the police would be visiting us at some point in the night.

'What should we do about Campbell?' I had asked my husband as my heart had fluttered with the thought of this house being infiltrated soon by officers in uniform.

'We need to keep him out of the way, obviously,' Karl had replied. 'We'll put him to bed and hope he stays up there.'

'But he'll wake up when he hears the noise,' I'd fired back. 'There's no way he'll sleep through if people come to our house. The cars outside on the street. The extra voices. The extra footsteps in our home. You know he's a light sleeper. He'll get out of bed and then what will we say to him? Sorry for waking you, baby, just ignore all these police and go back to sleep? Yeah, right.'

'Then what do you suggest? We keep him up so he can see his parents being questioned about a serious crime?'

'He won't understand what we're talking about,' I had hoped.

'You really want to put that to the test? If we're wrong, we'll be the reason he's in therapy when he's a teenager.'

'He'll be in therapy anyway if we get caught. But we might not, and maybe having him with us might help us.'

'How will it do that?'

'Think about it,' I had said then, only just thinking it through myself as I spoke. 'The police are coming here because they are suspicious of our family. They're looking for Darcy and they think my parents are hiding her from them. They'll most likely assume the same thing with us. That means they think we could be criminals, or at least the kind of people who take risks with the law. So what happens when they get here and see us with our four-year-old son? Do you think they'll assume we're criminals then? Or will they think we just look like normal parents trying to raise a child? It'll be the latter, and normal parents trying to raise a child don't really fit the profile of being criminals, do they?'

Karl agreed that I might have a point, and so it was set. We were keeping Campbell up for when the police arrived, and if any officer made a comment about our child being up unusually late, we would just tell the truth and say he had been off sick from kindergarten today, so this was not a typical day.

But keeping our son downstairs with us rather than out of sight up in his bedroom is also serving an even more powerful purpose than making us look like innocent, law-abiding citizens. The longer Karl and I sit here in the presence of our child – our child who is sweetly playing with his toys as if they are the most important thing in his little world – the more we are reminded of what is at stake. Neither one of us can afford to make a mistake when the police come because, if we do, this might be the last time we get to sit and watch our son play. One wrong word or one unintended facial expression, and the next time we see Campbell he could be a grown man who has learnt to hate his parents and never wants anything to do with them again.

Karl and I know what we need to do.

If we ever forget, we only need to look at the sleepy boy on the carpet to remember again.

It's twenty-seven minutes past midnight. I hear an unusual amount of noise out on the street.

'They're here,' comes the grim statement from my husband after he's gone to the window and glanced outside, and I quickly finish the last of the coffee in my cup before taking a deep breath and telling myself that it's show time.

'They're getting out of the cars,' Karl says next, but I don't need him to provide a running commentary, although he might just be doing it because he's nervous and doesn't know what else to do.

'Come away from the window,' I tell him. 'Let them knock on the door and then we'll go to see them.'

Karl does as I ask, which means we savour the peaceful ten seconds we get before we hear a thudding knock.

'I'll get it,' I offer, but Karl surprises me when he rushes to the door ahead of me, and while I initially think he's just being brave, I suddenly worry that he's changed his mind about this and is on his way to confess all to the police before the questions can even begin.

I linger in the lounge, with my son still playing by my feet, and listen nervously as the door opens and a man introduces himself as Detective Burgoyne. I recognise his voice and his name. He's the detective who was talking to my parents earlier. But as far as he's to know, this is the first time I've ever heard him speak.

I don't hear Karl crumbling and telling anybody that I am hiding things for my sister, nor that he and his son are in danger from my devious ways, so that is a huge relief. But there's not much time for relaxing because Detective Burgoyne enters the room, followed by an officer in uniform, and as soon as he sees the new arrivals, Campbell springs to his feet and starts pointing.

'Police! Police!' he cries, as excitable as he was when he saw them on TV earlier. But his enthusiasm for their appearance is not matched by his parents, and I see a very nervous-looking Karl follow the two men in, his shoulders hunched and one of his hands anxiously running over the stubble on his chin.

'We're sorry for the late intrusion,' the detective says before introducing himself. 'Who is this little man?'

'Campbell,' I say as I watch the detective shake Campbell's hand. But Campbell is more interested in the man in uniform behind the detective, and as he stares at the Chicago PD badge, I stare at the gun in his holster.

'How old is he?' Burgoyne asks.

'Four,' I reply as the detective looks at the sofa, and I extend a hand to let him know he can take a seat.

We all sit down, everyone except Campbell, who is still staring in awe at the policeman, but at least it keeps the atmosphere in this room relatively light, and I'm confident keeping our son up was worth it for this reason alone.

'Our son's been unwell today,' I say by way of explaining his late bedtime, and I notice Karl glance at me, the pair of us having already planned this part of the conversation, though it's much more daunting doing it for real.

'I hope you're feeling much better soon,' the detective says to Campbell, sounding very casual and relaxed – if only I was sitting in his seat rather than this one here.

'I suppose you'd like me to explain what is going on,' Burgoyne says, but I shake my head.

'It's okay. My parents called me a short time ago and told me you'd been to see them.'

'They did?'

'Yes,' I say, already lying, but this is a planned lie so I'm confident I can carry it off. But then I have a sudden crisis of confidence – this is a man who is paid to see through lies, so what if he already knows I'm misleading him? But it's too late for that, as I've already started, so I just have to go with it now. 'They told me you were looking for my sister.'

'That's correct. Do you know where she is?'

'No. As I'm sure my parents told you, she left unexpectedly one day and we haven't seen her since.'

'They did tell me that,' Burgoyne replies. 'But I was hoping you might be a little more helpful. Especially as you were with your sister when she was enquiring about the whereabouts of Eden Carthy at a nurse's reunion three months ago.'

'Eden?'

'Yes, your sister's former colleague and, I believe, she was a good friend of hers too. Did your parents care to mention what has become of her?'

'Erm...' I don't know how to answer that one but decide at the last second that I shouldn't try and lie.

'They said she's dead.'

'That's correct,' Burgoyne says, studying every inch of my face.

'It's awful. Do you know what happened to her?'

'We're gathering information, which is why it is important we speak to your sister,' Burgoyne explains. 'So if there is anything you can tell us about where she might be now, you need to do that. I believe your sister was looking for Eden before she went missing?'

'Well, yes, but she was looking for all sorts of people,' I quickly explain. 'She was trying to remember her life before her car accident. She was getting flashbacks, so she was trying to piece it all together. Memory loss is a terrible thing. My sister has been through an awful lot.'

I'm hoping the detective is feeling sorry for me and my family rather than suspicious of us, but he's probably far too experienced to let anything other than facts sway him. He turns to Karl now, who stiffens noticeably – not a good look on my husband's part.

'Is there anything you want to add, sir?' the detective asks my nervous husband.

He just shakes his head quickly, so at least he's not saying anything to make this worse.

'What if I can't find my sister?' I ask, knowing full well that I'm not even going to try and get her to come back to Chicago. 'If I can't find her, she won't be able to help.'

'Maybe we'll find her first,' comes Burgoyne's sinister reply, which makes me wonder if he's planning to go public with his search for my sister now that her family have proven to be of little use. That could mean photos of her being shown in the media, as well as details of our family being published online, which makes me feel very uncomfortable. But how would it make Darcy feel if she was to see the news? She'd be shocked and confused and probably very afraid. I don't want her to feel like that. That's why I hope she sticks to the advice I gave her in my notebook and avoids the news altogether. I also need to make sure that notebook never falls into the hands of the police because, if it did, they would know I was warning my sister to stay away, proving I knew everything about what she had done.

'I'm sorry we don't know where my sister is, but is there anything else we can do to help?' I ask the detective as my husband sits quietly beside me, fidgeting but mute.

'You could provide us with your fingerprints and a hair sample,' comes the chilling response.

'I'm sorry, what?' is all I can muster in reply.

'You're not under arrest so I can't legally make you provide them, but if you were willing to cooperate, it would be very helpful. Forensics are currently examining Eden's body, so that might give us some more clues about who she was in contact with at the time of her death. We're also looking in the same part of the lake for anything else and, if we find something, there may be clues there too. It could just save time if we had DNA samples for a person of interest all ready to go. Persons of interest like you and you sister, for example.'

Oh my god, he wants my DNA and fingerprints. Then he's going to find some of it on Eden and that will be it. I'll be arrested for her murder and, if I keep protecting Darcy, I'll get blamed for all of this.

'You can take my fingerprints!' Campbell cries, holding out his hands to the detective, which gets a chuckle from the officer in uniform, but I'm not laughing. Neither is my husband. In fact, he's gone very pale. What are we going to do? What can I say?

'I've not done anything wrong, so if I'm not under arrest I don't wish to provide anything,' I say, using the detective's information against him, and he stares at me for a long beat before nodding.

'Okay, well, I'm sure we'll be talking again, but until then have a lovely evening and do let me know if you remember anything about your sister's whereabouts that might be helpful to us.'

The detective and the police officer stand to leave, and Campbell looks sad to see them go. Unlike his parents, who are breathing a sigh of relief, albeit a very temporary one. That's because I know this can only end one way now if the police don't drop my family as suspects.

They'll eventually want DNA samples, and they'll possibly search my parents' home too. If so, they're bound to find something connecting us to Eden, and if they find Laurence's body, they might find something connecting me to him too.

So I have no choice now.

I have to leave before they come back here to arrest me.

THIRTY-FOUR

DARCY

The dream I'm having is a vivid one. I can see my sister in front of me. We're in our playroom, the one in our family home, the one our parents designed for us so we had somewhere to put all our toys and let our imaginations run wild. This is our room, mine and my sister's, and we love it in here. Most of all, we love being with each other. We're best friends and we spend all our free time in each other's company. We're only young, so we have a lot of time to share. We don't understand the adult world yet. We don't know what jobs are or how useful money can be or the stresses and strains that older people are under every day. All we know is that we love playtime and, as my sister passes me a doll in a pink dress, I smile because this is all I want to do.

Sometimes we fight. Pippa can be annoying. She says I can be too. We don't always play well together. Occasionally, we squabble. But I still love her, and I know that she loves me. Most of all, I know that we will always be together.

Suddenly we're older and all the toys have vanished. All the colour drains from the walls too and the magical playroom in our parents' home is replaced by a cold, dark basement devoid of anything pleasant – and now I feel scared. Pippa seems to be getting further away too, like there's a widening distance between us and, when I try to grab her, she slips out of reach. I try to call to her, but no words leave my mouth and, suddenly, my sister has gone, leaving me alone and afraid in this awful room without windows.

I'm not alone for long. Somebody else is here. I can see them, lying in the bed in the corner of the room, so I make my way over to them, my feet shuffling slowly over the concrete until I see who it is. It's a woman I recognise, a former patient, I think, someone I used to care for. Her name is on the tip of my tongue, but just escapes me, though it's not important. What is important is what she has to say to me.

'Help me,' she whispers.

I don't know how to do that, though I want to find out, so I go to take a step closer but, as I do, a strong hand holds me back. I turn and see him, the man I've also seen before, and he tells me he will take over from here.

'Laurence, no, please don't do this,' the woman in the bed says, but he ignores her and brings a syringe to her arm, the needle almost coming into contact with her skin.

I feel a tear running down my cheek. I know I should stop this. I know this woman will die if I don't.

But I do nothing, and now she's dead.

Only then do I scream.

'Hey! It's okay!' the voice in my ear says, and I open my eyes to see a concerned face beside me. It's Irene, and she is trying to let me know that it was simply a bad dream. Only when I get my bearings do I realise that she is right. Of course it was a dream. I've had that dream before, or at least some version of it. But now I'm back in the basement and the reality of my current situation returns to me.

We're still trapped down here.

Parker still has us under lock and key.

'Are you okay?' Irene asks me as I get to my feet and stretch my legs, feeling a stiffness in my neck and also feeling surprised that I was able to drift off.

'How long was I asleep?' I ask before remembering that it's a stupid question to ask – we have no way of knowing how much time is passing down here.

'I don't know. A while, I guess,' Irene says. 'I fell asleep too, but I woke before you. I had a bad dream too. They're pretty common down here, unfortunately.'

My fellow prisoner seems to think that nightmares are just a consequence of being locked away in here, but I know different.

I know my nightmares started before I was in here.

More than that, I know my nightmares aren't just nightmares.

'They're not dreams,' I say to Irene as I slowly walk around the claustrophobic basement. 'I think they're flashbacks.'

'Flashbacks? Of what?'

'I don't know. Things I've done in my past,' I say, hesitating before adding the next part. 'Things I've done wrong.'

Irene doesn't understand what I'm getting at, but why should she? We've only just met and she's far more worried about the person keeping us in here than the person she's in with. But maybe that's where she's making a mistake and, more importantly, maybe it's linked to where Parker is making a mistake too.

'I think I've done some bad things in my past,' I confess, though I'm only assuming based on the flashbacks and dreams. 'I think that's why my family sent me away. I think it's why I can't watch the news. I must have done something wrong and, if I'm guessing right, and the heavy feeling of guilt I carry on a daily basis is real, I think I watched a woman die and didn't do anything to help her.'

Irene looks shocked, and confused, as she should be, but I try and turn this into a positive.

'I guess I don't know what I'm fully capable of,' I go on. 'But maybe that's a good thing. It means Parker won't know either.'

Then I pause before saying something that might sound dramatic, but could also be the frightening truth.

'What if he's not the most dangerous person in this house?' I ask Irene. 'What if I am?'

Irene doesn't respond, but I don't need her to. All I need is to use this potential boost of confidence in a productive way, so I start walking up the staircase to the locked door to try and do just that.

'What are you doing?' Irene asks me, and I look back to see her reach the bottom of the staircase, though she is not following me up.

'I'm going to try and get us out of here,' I reply calmly, ignoring the nervous tension in my body that grows with each ascending step I make.

'It's pointless! The door's locked!' Irene calls after me, as if I'm not aware that Parker turned the key in the lock when he closed this door. I can't just sit down in the basement and do nothing, so as I reach the door I try the handle.

It doesn't turn, as I expected. So now I'm going to start being disruptive.

'Open this door!' I call out, pounding my fists into the barrier between us and freedom, trying to make as much noise as I can. Maybe if I can keep the noise up, Parker might worry that someone outside the house might hear me. Though it might be unlikely given how big his grounds are and how far it is to the neighbouring property, I have to try something. If all I do is give Parker a headache, it has to be better than letting him think we're not going to put up a fight.

I keep calling out, begging for help, calling Parker some nasty names, and basically telling him that he isn't going to get away with this, though none of it has any effect on the door opening. Irene keeps telling me to stop, but I ignore her. If she's been down here for a month then she isn't the best person to take advice from about getting out. After several minutes, I take a break to get my breath back and give my hands a rest, but when I do I hear something.

It's the television.

Is Parker just casually watching TV as if he doesn't have two prisoners in the basement?

I press my ear to the door and keep listening, unable to believe the gall of this man. Then I hear what he is watching. It sounds like a news report.

'*Good morning, America. Here are the latest headlines around the country.*'

That reporter's voice tells me what part of the day we are in and now I know it's morning, I realise we've been in here all night.

'It's the morning,' I call down to Irene, figuring it might help keep us sane if we have some sense of which part of the day it is, not that it makes too much difference to our plight.

I try and hear what else is being said on TV, but I'm struggling now. Has Parker turned the volume down? Maybe he has. It's just another way to frustrate me. But I'm far from finished getting my frustrations out.

I start banging on the door again and call out Parker's name, as well as several threats about how he won't get away with this, and how things will be much worse if the police come here and find us in his basement. But I don't think the police are coming, and Parker clearly believes this too, or he would let us go before things got worse.

Irene keeps telling me to stop, almost as if the noise I'm making is causing her more distress than it's causing Parker, which is clearly not my intention, but it seems to be what's happening. Just as I am about to stop, I hear a key turning.

up to, Darcy? Are they the dangerous ones here or is that you?'

'If you think I'm dangerous then you should let me go,' I say, feigning confidence. 'Before I hurt you.'

I wonder if that will have any impact on my captor, but when he laughs I get my answer.

'Let you go? No way. Not until I find out what it is that you're connected to in Chicago,' Parker says with an excited grin. 'I'm going to keep watching the news and see what happens. This could be really big. What if the police are looking for you and I can hand you over on a platter? There might be a reward! I could be doing them a favour in catching you! Wouldn't that be ironic?'

Parker winks before leaving, closing the door behind himself, locking it and then, presumably, going back to watch the news. I wish I could get up and climb the stairs again, but I'm in too much pain to move quickly. And now I know what happens if I do get to the top, I'm in no rush to try it again.

'I'm sorry,' I say to Irene, who has moved away from me and is now standing in the corner. 'I should have listened to you. I shouldn't have banged on the door.'

I hope Irene might accept my apology, or at least smile to show me that she is still on my side. But she doesn't do any of that. Instead, she's looking like she wishes she was alone again.

Parker's story about the news must have spooked her, and she's wondering who I am and what I have done. I'll have made that worse with what I told her before she came in here. My references to my dreams and flashbacks and my fear that I have done something bad in my past must seem even worse now after what Parker has said.

'Whatever is going on out there,' I say tentatively, because I don't fully understand it myself so I can't expect Irene to, 'I want you to know that it has nothing to do with what is going on in here. We still need to get out of this basement and save ourselves, and we have to stick together to do that. You understand me?'

Irene stays very still as I wait for her to answer me, but finally she nods, albeit with little conviction.

'Can you help me up?' I ask her, grimacing as I try to get off the floor.

Irene hesitates before coming to my aid, and she helps me to my feet, which is not a particularly pleasant experience when everything aches. I'm not going to be moving fast for a while, that's obvious, but that's also a huge problem – speed might be the one thing that could have helped me in this situation.

'We need to try and overpower him when he opens the door again,' I say once Irene has helped me to the nearest wall and I lean against it.

'It won't work,' is the reply, but that's no good.

'We have to try,' I say again. 'He must be bringing us some food soon. He hasn't fed me since I've been in here.'

My rumbling stomach is testament to that, although with so much to worry about, food is fairly low on my list of priorities. I know my energy levels will continue to dip without any sustenance, though maybe that's Parker's plan. He'll wait until I'm weak like Irene before he gives me anything, at which point I'll just be so grateful that my will to fight might have left me.

I'm so thirsty too, but there isn't any sign of water coming either. At one point, a while ago, I thought that might be a blessing, because it would mean there was less chance of having to use the bowl in the corner of the room that Irene has obviously been using for her waste disposal, but now I would put my thirst above any embarrassment.

'We can't give up,' is all I can say to Irene as I touch a few parts of my torso, seeing where the most tender spots are, but I must look incredibly weak and vulnerable, so it can't be adding any weight to my words. Before I can say anything more, the door unexpectedly opens again and Parker reappears, looking down at us and noting that we have moved since he last came in here, not that it matters much.

'The plot thickens,' he says with another smug grin, and I have no idea what he means, but I have a feeling I'm about to find out.

'Breaking news from Chicago,' he goes on, still grinning. 'The police have found another body in the lake. It's a man this time, and people are speculating that it might be Laurence, the guy who has been missing for three months. You know anything about that, Darcy? Or are the police going to have to visit your family again to get some answers?'

THIRTY-SIX

PIPPA

It's been precisely eighteen minutes since I saw the breaking news report that told me and anybody else watching that a man's body had been discovered in Lake Michigan, not far from where Eden's body had been found previously. I don't know how long it's going to be until they confirm the identity of that male, but for me and my family, it's not something we need to wait for. We already know who it is and that's why we need to make plans to get ahead of this situation.

I've already told my husband what needs to happen next.

Now I need to tell my parents.

The conversation I am about to have with them is one that would be best to hold in person, but I've decided that it will have to take place over the phone instead. I'm paranoid that there might be an undercover police officer lurking outside my home and, if they see me speed towards my parents' place, they might think that is suspicious. I assume they haven't tapped the phone lines, so calls are safer than in-person meetings, and that's what I'll go with now.

'Pick up the damn phone,' I say under my breath as I head into my son's bedroom, trying to figure out what we need to take with us and what can be left behind. Campbell is downstairs having his breakfast and, as of yet, doesn't know that his life is about to be turned upside down. But he will do soon enough, especially when he sees me coming back downstairs with a bag full of his belongings, a bag that might not contain some of his favourite toys as we can't take them all.

'Pippa?' Dad says as he answers the phone, and I'm relieved to hear his voice – if he's answering, it means the police aren't there yet.

'Dad! Listen to me! They found Laurence's body, so he won't be a suspect in Eden's death! That means they're going to be looking at Darcy again, and that means they'll be coming back there, so you need to pack up and get out. You and Mom! You need to go now, before they do a proper search and find Eden's DNA in your study or our DNA on the body. I know Mom cleaned the study, but it'll be no match for a team of forensics!'

That's an awful lot of information to throw at my father, and I did it all at a fast pace, but there is no time for anything less.

'I've seen the news,' Dad grimly confirms. 'And I expect the police will be even more interested in finding Darcy now.'

'Yes, they will! Darcy is connected to both those people and she's missing too, so the police will be all over us. We have to get out of here before they formally take us to the station for official statements. And before they search our homes! We have to go now before it's too late!'

'What are you suggesting? We just run?'

'Yes! We run now before they come back! I'm packing already!'

'You're what?'

Dad is stunned, and I hear Mom's voice in the background of the call, and he tells her what I've just told him. There's no time for them to debate this. If the police come back before they've left, they'll be stuck, and if that study gets examined and a single drop of Eden's blood is found within the carpet fibres, we'll all go to prison for a very long time.

'We can't just leave,' Dad says, but I have something that might persuade him.

'Well, I'm going. And I'm taking Campbell with me, so if you want to see either of us again, you'll come with us!' I cry, which is harsh – it's emotional blackmail, and I hate using such a thing on my parents, but it's surely the fastest trick I can deploy.

'Pippa, slow down,' Dad tries, but that's all he says before I hear Mom telling him to give her the phone. I hear them arguing, so I spend the time throwing bundles of Campbell's clothes into a suitcase, then Mom comes on the line.

'Pippa, wait. I agree that we might need to leave, but there's a problem if we do,' she says.

'What? Money? You've got loads of that, and the rest we can figure out on the road,' I reply without pausing the packing.

'I'm not talking about money,' Mom cries. 'I'm talking about Darcy. How will she ever find us if we leave? What if she comes back one day to look for us and we're gone?'

I stop what I'm doing and think about what Mom has just said. She's right. If we leave Chicago, the address I left in my sister's notebook would be useless. She shouldn't ever come back here, especially now that the police are onto her and us, but if she ever did and we were gone, we'd be separated forever.

'No, wait, it's fine, I could write to her and tell her where we have moved to!' I cry when it comes to me. 'I know her address in Florida, so I'll write to her and tell her we had to leave Chicago and start somewhere new. I'll explain everything and maybe we can all be together again in the new place, but right now, we really have to get going!'

'Pippa!' calls my husband's voice from downstairs, and now he's vying for my attention too, but I'm not finished with my parents yet. I can't hang up until I know they're going to start packing too, otherwise I may never see them again.

'We can't just leave. This is our home,' Dad says, and I guess he's wrestled the phone back off Mom. It's hard enough talking to one of them without them passing the phone back and forth between each other, but the content of my message won't change whoever I'm talking to.

'If you want to risk it then stay, but I'm going!'

'Wait!' I hear Mom call out in the background, which means Dad probably has the call on speaker. 'We'll pack now. Where shall we meet you? Shall we come to you?'

'No, just get out of the house and I'll call you when we're out,' I say, relieved they are coming with us, because I'll need all their assistance, not to mention their money, or at least what we can get of it before the police potentially freeze their assets.

'Pippa!'

Karl is calling me again, and this time I can respond to him because my parents have now agreed, so I tell them to hurry up and then end the call.

'What?' I cry out as I leave my son's bedroom with a heavy suitcase of his belongings in tow.

'The news is getting crazy. It's on every channel. Everyone in Chicago must be talking about this now!' he tells me.

'That's why we need to go,' I shout as I head down the stairs, the suitcase banging off the wall. 'Before they start talking about us.'

'I don't know if I can do this,' Karl says, which is utterly unhelpful at this late stage.

'What?'

'I don't know if I can leave. What if we stay? Maybe we'll be okay?'

'Are you crazy? The police have already been here once and they've found another body since then. Why wouldn't they come back? It's only a matter of time until Darcy's photo is on the news and, once people are looking for her, our photo will be on there too.'

'I didn't sign up for any of this,' Karl says, shaking his head and looking on the verge of a breakdown.

'You married me and, right now, this is what you've got!' I cry. 'Either you come with me, or you watch me and Campbell leave. But we are going, with or without you!'

I fear that Karl is going to do something stupid like grab hold of our son and say that he's not going anywhere. What would I do if that happened? I've already hurt somebody who threatened my family's safety. Could I hurt my husband to stop him taking my son?

I don't have to find out the answer to that awful dilemma because Karl snaps out of it and runs upstairs to grab some more things. That leaves me to go and check on Campbell. I find him with his head in his hands beside a bowl of soggy cereal. He has no idea how serious the situation is, but he is not stupid and knows that something is wrong, hence his unhappy demeanour.

'I'm sorry, darling, but we have to go,' I say to him.

'Where are we going?'

'We're going to go on vacation, and Granny and Grandpa are coming too,' I say, which I hope will make him feel better about leaving behind his friends at kindergarten, not to mention all his home comforts. 'Does that sound like fun?'

Campbell thinks about it, but he does something that makes me fearful.

He shakes his head. And while it's only a simple action from an innocent child, it feels like so much more.

It feels ominous.

Like my son, even at his tender age, knows better than me.

He knows that whatever we do, this is not going to end well.

THIRTY-SEVEN

DARCY

I wish I could hurt someone with the strength of my eyes alone. If so, and looks really could kill, Parker would be dead already. I've certainly been glaring at him long enough to do some serious damage. Unfortunately, that's not how this works. I can look at him with hate and venom all I want to, but he remains entirely unaffected by it. Or maybe he's taking strength from it, which is the exact opposite of my intention.

He's still standing at the top of the stairs while I am down below, in this basement, holding my aching sides and wishing I was strong enough to charge at him, knock him down and get out of this house. Irene is to my left, looking just as useless as I feel, and that's it. The three of us, one with the upper hand, and the other two with little help or hope.

'You're not going to tell me why the police were at the address in your notebook?' Parker asks me once more, but the answer remains the same. I shake my head, because I can't, though he thinks it's because I won't.

While I think that should end his fun, he seems intent on staying here and fishing around for more information, as if he has access to a treasure trove full of it that the media and the Chicago police would love to have.

'Come on, if you ever want to get out of here, you've got to do better than that,' he says, but just before any more can be said, all three of us hear something that none of us were expecting.

It's the sound of a window breaking.

Parker's face drops, which tells me he was not expecting that, and why would he? It didn't sound like something positive. At least not for him as the homeowner. But for his two prisoners, it might just be the most amazing sound we've ever heard.

Is somebody else here?

Irene and I take one look at each other and decide to find out.

'HELP!' we both cry in unison. 'HELP US! WE'RE IN HERE!'

Parker reacts to our sudden shouting by rushing out of the basement and slamming the door shut, no doubt to keep our loud voices contained within. If somebody is here, there's no way we are going to do as he wants and stay quiet – this might be the only chance we get.

'HELP!' I shout as Irene rushes up the stairs, suddenly changing her opinion about how valuable it is to try that. I watch as she reaches the door and starts banging on it, and I slowly make my way up behind her, clutching my sorest rib and breathing heavily, but determined to help my fellow prisoner if there is a chance.

I reach her as Irene's banging intensifies and I keep calling out, the pair of us working together to make as much noise as possible. We're both stunned into silence when the door flings open, and we see who is standing on the other side of it.

It's not Parker this time.

It's his father.

'Joe?' I ask as I stare at the man I last saw when I left his apartment after a day of caring for him. 'What are you doing here?'

I look behind him, fearful that his son might be about to appear and ruin any hopes I might have of this being good news, but he just shakes his head.

'Don't worry about my son,' he tells me and Irene. 'Come on, let's get you both out of here.'

He gestures for us to follow him, and we don't need any more inviting, so together – with Irene walking out first as she's been in here much longer than me – we leave the basement.

I've never been so happy to see a kitchen before but, as I look around, I'm not looking for items of furniture.

I'm looking for Parker.

Where is he?

'What happened?' I ask Joe. 'Where's your son? Are we safe?'

Irene looks just as fearful as me, and she's probably just as aware as I am that there would be nothing crueller than us two escaping the basement only for something terrible to happen next. But Joe doesn't look as pensive.

'He's in there,' he says, pointing in the direction of another room, before I notice that there are a couple of drops of blood on his shirt sleeve.

'Is that your blood?' I ask Joe nervously, and he looks at it before shaking his head.

I'm guessing that means the blood belongs to his son, but I won't know for sure unless I go and check, so I tentatively head in the direction that Joe just pointed. As I leave the kitchen and enter the lounge, I find the man I'm looking for. Parker is lying on the carpet and there's more blood around him. He's face down and not moving, which is lovely to see, though very shocking. I have lots of questions. I also see the broken window in the lounge, which only gives me more questions. But it's Irene who asks the first one.

'Is he dead?' she wants to know and, coincidentally, that would have been my next question too.

'I think so,' Joe replies, and while that sounds like good news, I'm reminded that we're talking about this man's son. Irene doesn't seem too bothered, and she immediately kicks at Parker's body, letting out her frustration on the man who kept her imprisoned for so long. But as glad as I am to be out, I can't let her attack Parker's body while his father stands by, so I pull her away and tell her that it's over now.

She's crying and I have tears in my eyes too, but when I look at Joe, I see he is the same.

'I don't understand,' I say to him when Irene has calmed down. 'What happened? What are you doing here?'

'You didn't come to work today,' he replies simply. 'So I thought something was wrong.'

Joe looks weak again now, fading from the man he was when he opened the basement door and, I'm guessing, the man he was when he attacked Parker, so I invite him to take a seat in the kitchen where he doesn't have to look at the body.

He accepts the invite and, once he's seated, he explains some more.

'I'm so sorry,' he says, fighting back tears, but he's looking at Irene this time rather than me. 'I should have stopped him sooner. I knew something was wrong when I hadn't seen you for a while and, when I asked Parker, he joked that you were locked up in the basement. But that wasn't funny to me because when he was younger, he had a fascination with news stories about being people trapped. In caves, in houses, in cars, whatever it was he seemed to derive pleasure from the thought of somebody being stuck. I thought it was just a silly childhood phase, but I realised it might not be a joke when I noticed him start to get more anxious to get home, as if he had something to get back for. I asked him about you several more times and each answer got stranger and stranger before he told me to not talk to him about you at all, that nobody could help you now. I was terrified what he meant by that, so I was too scared to ask. But I should have done more. I could have helped you. I'm so sorry.'

That's the confirmation, not that I needed it at this point, that Joe had some idea of what his son was doing with his ex-girlfriend. Then, after he hinted about it to me so that I might investigate, he obviously realised something might have gone wrong when I didn't arrive for work.

'So you came here to help us?' I ask, and Joe nods.

'I haven't been here for a while,' he admits. 'I got a taxi and I have the keycode to the gate written on a piece of paper in my wallet, so I got through the gates. All the doors were locked. So I broke a window.'

'Thank goodness you did!' Irene cries, clearly not mad at him for not helping sooner – he's a vulnerable man who has probably been just as afraid of Parker as we have.

'How did you hurt him?' I ask next, because it needs asking. Parker is a much younger and stronger man than his father, so surely Joe wouldn't have easily overpowered him.

'I hit him with my hammer,' Joe says, and that was not what I was expecting.

'A hammer?'

'Yeah. I brought it from home. I took it from my toolbox. I told the taxi driver I was returning it to my son. I thought I might need it.'

I peer back into the lounge and notice the handle of the hammer poking out from beneath the sofa beside where Parker lies, and it's certainly the kind of weapon that could overcome a size-and-strength disadvantage.

'We need to call the police!' Irene says then as if that's the right thing to do. Maybe it is, but not for me.

'No, no police,' I say adamantly.

'Why not? That man locked me away for a month and he

locked you away too! The world needs to hear what he did to us! And it needs to hear what a hero Joe is for saving us!'

'It's not as simple as that,' I say, and I'm not just thinking of myself here. 'What will you tell the police, Joe? You'll probably be arrested. If you brought the weapon here, they might say it was premeditated.'

'I don't care about that,' he says with a simple shrug, looking every bit as sad as a man who's done what he's done should. 'I won't remember who I am in a year or two, so it doesn't matter what happens to me. If I do go to prison, at least I'll be cared for.'

As crazy as it sounds, Joe probably has a point. He does need somebody to look after him, and a prison hospital might not be the worst place in the world to get that help. But he deserves better, although sadly, like many people, his health won't let things get better.

'I get that you need to call the police,' I say, looking at Irene and feeling sorry for everything she's been through. 'But I can't be here when they arrive.'

She stares at me and gets what I am saying. I had told her about the flashbacks and hinted at my dark past, and she'd heard Parker taunting me with news about the drama in Chicago and how it might be connected to me. So she gets it. She knows this is how it has to be for me.

'I wish you all the best,' I say to her as I give her a hug, and while we can only embrace gingerly thanks to my injuries and her exhaustion, it's still a pleasant embrace between two survivors. Then I turn to Joe.

'Thank you,' I say. 'Thank you for doing the right thing. I know how hard it must have been for you.'

Joe has a tear on his cheek, and I take care to wipe it away for him before I turn to leave.

'There's a key there,' Joe says, pointing to a hook by the back door, helpful for me to get out of here. Before I go, I look for one more thing.

My notebook is sitting on the kitchen table, and I pick it up and check inside that all the pages are still intact. They are, so with it back in my possession, I head for the door, using the key to open it before stepping outside and feeling the freedom of the fresh air on my face.

I limp down the long driveway to the gate, one hand still on my aching ribs, and as I reach it the gate automatically slides open. Maybe there was a sensor on this side, or maybe Joe opened it from the house for me. The gate slides fully open and now I'm out on the street, each step I take moving me further away from the horrible person who owns the house behind me.

I need to go home now, and my apartment is my next stop.

But that's not home. Not my real home.

My real home is Chicago.

That's where my family are.

And by the sounds of it, they need me.

THIRTY-EIGHT

PIPPA

No one on the run ever wants to stop, but sometimes you have no choice.

Particularly if there's a child with you.

Campbell has been moaning about needing to go to the toilet for the last half an hour and, despite me telling him to wait, there comes a point when that won't work anymore. If that was all it was about, we could have stopped by the side of a quiet road somewhere and he could have done his business behind a bush. But we need to stop for another reason too. We have some food but we could surely use more, and now we can see a service station coming into view, it seems like a good time to make that stop. But it'll have to be a quick one.

'You take him to the bathroom,' I tell Karl, who is sitting to my left, on the other side of our son, who is in between us. We're in the back of the five-seater car that my father bought with cash several hours ago, and he's at the wheel now while my mother is sitting next to him in the front. We've been heading north out of Chicago all day, our luggage in the trunk and our minds on whether or not what we're doing is going to work in the long-term. The truth is we don't know if our plan is going to be successful because, if we are at the centre of a huge media storm and the subject of a large police hunt, our odds are slim, but at least we know where we are going.

Our destination is Minnesota, or more specifically, a remote part of that state full of sprawling forests and mountain ranges. We're going there because not only is it remote, which is ideal, but Dad knows of a specific place where we could stay while we lie low and figure out our next move. We'd been in the car for less than ten minutes this morning when Dad told us what he knew.

'A guy I worked with years ago used to hire a cabin up in Minnesota during the holidays,' he told us as we sped out of Chicago, moving against all the early morning traffic that was heading into the city. 'He loved it up there. Said it was really tranquil, even with a few of the other cabins nearby. But one year, he stopped going. The company who owned the cabins went bust and they were no longer available for holiday rentals. My colleague said what a shame it was because they were all just sitting empty now.'

'That's where we're going?' Karl had asked sceptically. 'You think they're still empty now?'

'Have you got any better ideas?' Dad had snapped back, plainly in no mood for trouble, and my husband had wisely not said anything after that.

The truth was that Dad's plan sounded like it could potentially work. It was definitely the best option we had. We needed to go somewhere remote and, if the cabins were there, empty but still in some kind of reasonable working order, they would make a great place for us to hide out. My parents had withdrawn as much cash as they could before we left the city as soon as the banks opened, as did Karl and I, which was a sizeable amount when put together, so I wasn't worried about us running out of funds for a while. However, according to Dad, there is less of a need for money where we are going, and more of a need for hunting and survival skills, so cash might be pretty useless anyway when trying to trap an animal and cook it on an open fire. But forget money or hunting or even the cold weather when winter sets in, if we're still on the run at that point. What I am really worried about is anybody figuring out where we have gone.

Unfortunately, that is always going to be part of life on the run. The constant looking over the shoulder. The never-ending paranoia that somebody might recognise you and the awful dread in the pit of your stomach that you've made a mistake that there is no coming back from.

I am experiencing all those things now as Dad steers us off the highway and into the service station parking lot and, already, my eyes are on the other cars here and, more specifically, the people who might own them. If anybody remembers us and mentions it to the police at a later date, that could help them narrow down their search area, so we need to make sure we blend in seamlessly to the background.

No sooner have we got out of the car than Campbell starts screaming.

'Campbell! *Ssshhh!*' I say quietly, my eyes scanning the parking lot, but nobody else is out here and looking in our direction. 'What is it?'

'I really need to go!' he cries, and I realise that it's going to be a rush for the bathroom. His dad does too, so he picks up our son and jogs with him to the building while I hang back with my parents.

Dad instantly puts the radio on and tries to find a news bulletin, and I'm glad he's doing it now that my son is out of the car so he can't hear if our names are being mentioned. But Dad's not having much luck so far, probably because the signal isn't great here, and I guess it's only going to get worse the further into remote Minnesota we go.

'I'll go inside and see if there are any TVs showing the news,' I suggest, not just because that will help with that particular problem, but because it will get me closer to my husband and son, who I am worried about being out of sight for too long.

'Be careful,' Mom says as I walk away from the car and, by that, she means don't let anybody get too good a look at my face, just in case.

I put up my hood on my jacket to help with that, as well as keep my head bowed when I see a couple of people walking my way. I pass them but keep my eyes on the blacktop, and I doubt they even noticed me. I just need to keep it that way when I go inside, where I expect there will be a lot more people than out here.

Sure enough, I'm right, and as I enter the building there must be at least twenty other people in here. Most of them are motorists or their passengers, sitting at tables, eating fast food or queuing to buy snacks before getting back on the road. There are some employees here too, their bored-looking faces staring out from behind various counters, and I make sure not to let my gaze linger too long on them, because that would be an unusual thing to do. Instead, I look around for what I need, and I see it in the corner beside a burger joint.

There's a large flatscreen TV hanging on the wall.

And it's showing the news.

I grit my teeth as I wait for an update on events in Chicago, but for a brief and blissful moment, there is a second when I think that we could be overreacting by running. Maybe it's not such a big deal. Perhaps the police already have something else to distract them. What if the world is already moving on and those bodies will forever remain part of an unsolved mystery?

The problem with wishful thinking is that, inevitably,

reality reminds the person doing it that the world doesn't work that way.

That's certainly what happens when I see my parents' home appear on screen.

I stare at the familiar property, the one where my mother would always be found baking in the kitchen while Dad would be working on something in his study, but there's no sense of comfort to be found in these images now. Not with all the police cars on the driveway and yellow 'crime scene' tape strung across the front door.

The volume on this TV is low but the subtitles are on, and that's how I'm able to find out what is going on back in that quiet suburb of Chicago.

'A local resident has come forward and reported a woman matching Eden's description in the vicinity of Sherwood Crescent, prompting the police to return to a place already of interest. This house in Winnetka was visited by officers shortly after Eden's body was found. But now they're back and this time they have found something.'

It's as if all the air is sucked out of me. They've found something? What is it?

Then I see Detective Burgoyne on screen, talking to reporters, and he's more than happy to tell anybody watching what it is.

'A forensic search of the property behind me has indicated that Eden Carthy was in the house and she was injured,' he says as I get confirmation that it's as bad as it could be. *'We are now urgently seeking the owners of the property, Dr Adrian and Scarlett Miller, to come forward to assist with our enquiries. We are also seeking the whereabouts of their two daughters, Darcy Miller and Pippa Simpson. The former has not been seen for some time and is wanted for questioning.'*

'Mommy!'

I turn around and see Campbell running towards me, his

arms out wide in anticipation of me taking him in a hug. But this sweet moment between parent and child is ruined by my fear that he is being too loud, drawing too much attention to us and somebody is going to remember that we were here.

'We need to go,' I say to Karl as he quickly catches up to our son, and as I make sure to keep Campbell's body facing away from the TV screen, my husband gets a good look at it and understands the seriousness of the situation.

'They're looking for us already?' he asks nervously, and I nod.

'All of us,' I confirm before I tell him to pick up our son so we can get out of here as quickly as possible. He does that while Campbell moans about not wanting to get back in the car yet. But I ignore him as we go to leave, though there's one thing I can't ignore.

Despite knowing it might not do me any good, I can't resist taking one last glance at the TV screen.

When I do, I see my sister's face staring back at me.

Her photo on the news confirms the police are looking for her, but I know what I have to do. I have to find her first. My initial priority is making sure my son is safe, so I will go with my family to the cabin and hide out until we're settled. But I can't stay there because the family isn't complete without Darcy with us. Therefore, I'll have to leave everyone else behind to go and get her.

It seems an impossible task, locating my sister safely while in the swarm of a media and police frenzy, but I have to try. I also have the feeling she'll return to Chicago. Call it a sibling sixth sense, but I just know it. I told her to avoid the news, but it'll surely become impossible. She's bound to catch a glimpse of her face on the front cover of a newspaper, or worse, somebody is bound to recognise her and possibly point her out to the police, forcing my sister to run. When she does, she'll go where anybody goes when they feel threatened.

She'll go home.

I know she'll be looking for me, just like I'm going to be looking for her.

Now I have to believe that we'll find each other again.

Before it's too late.

THIRTY-NINE

DARCY

The small rucksack by my feet holds everything I own in this world, which happens to be a few items of clothing, some toiletry accessories and, of course, my trusty notebook. It's not much, and it's certainly less luggage than some of the other people sitting on the seats around me have.

I've kept my eyes mostly on the floor in front of me ever since I sat down here about an hour ago, but I glance up now to check the departure screen. When I do, I see that there's now only sixteen minutes until my bus departs. I have a ticket on a service heading north and, while my ultimate destination is Chicago, it's going to take me a while to get there. It's certainly going to take me longer than if I was to fly, but I've decided that cross-country buses are a better option for me at this time.

I've decided that based on what the news is saying.

To the left of the departure screen is a standard television and it's showing the national news, which is providing the dozen or so passengers I'm sitting with some form of entertainment while we wait for our transport to be ready. That news broadcast has been showing me some things that have been making me feel very uncomfortable while I've been sitting here, so I'd rather it be turned off. Unfortunately, I don't think it will be. That means any moment now, I'm about to see my image on screen one more time.

Limping home from Parker's place after a very torrid time there, I had only stopped on the way to glance at the TV screens in a café to get a news update. When I had, I'd seen images of that man from my flashbacks.

Laurence. His body had been found. And, apparently, it had something to do with me.

I also heard references to what Parker had already told me. The police had visited an address in Winnetka, Chicago, as part of their investigation, and it matched the address in my notebook. I'd rushed back to my apartment and started to pack after that, my mind already made up that I was going to head back to where my notebook said I was from. I'd already broken the first rule in it, which was to avoid the news, so it didn't seem a big leap to go ahead and break the second one too. It wasn't as if I had much to lose. My life in Florida was a mess, as evidenced by the fact that I'd escaped a locked basement and seen a dead body all before breakfast this morning. I figured I should go back to Chicago and find out what I had done in my past, whatever it may be, even at the risk of being arrested. But by the time I'd arrived at this bus station and purchased a ticket, I started to get a sense that it was bad.

Really, really bad.

How do you know you're in trouble? Usually, when your photo is shown on national news during a report about a police investigation into a double homicide. That's a pretty good indication that things aren't good, and that's the exact indication I got when I saw myself flash up on the TV screen beside the departures notices.

The first thing I did was stop breathing for a few seconds – it was a frightening thing to see.

The second thing I did was look around to see if anybody else had realised that it was me.

Fortunately, everyone in the bus station had their heads down, their eyes on phones, over newspapers, or on their bags to make sure they didn't lose them. Most people who travel cross-country this way are doing so out of necessity rather than desire, so whatever they do have in their possession matters greatly to them. I've mostly kept my head down ever since, though it's been hard to do that when I seem to be a character of the main news story in the country.

It got even harder when it seemed I wasn't the only one.

The three names in my notebook are important to me, not just because the titles next to them are Mom, Dad and Sister, but because they've been the only real companion I've had since I've been in Florida. Looking at my notebook every morning before facing the day, and every night before ending it, has given me a sort of comfort, one I haven't been able to find anywhere else since I've mostly been alone here. I feel like I should know these people, and I guess that I do, or at least used to, but even though I can't specifically remember my past with them, they are my family and that means I should help them.

By the looks of things, they need it.

I'm not the only one the police are looking for. Mine is not the only image on the news. There have been three more photos shown featuring persons of interest, and they all match the names in my notebook.

Scarlett. Adrian. Pippa.

The police aren't just looking for me.

They are looking for all of us.

I'd be lying if I said I wasn't afraid of what might be waiting for me in Chicago. But I'd also be lying if I didn't feel like I had a duty to my family to make sure they are okay. They're obviously in as much trouble as I am, and while I can't remember what it is we've done, it must be big if everyone in Chicago is looking for us.

This is not a time for us to be apart.

We need to be together.

So I need to find my family before it's too late.

There are now only nine minutes to go until my bus departs, and while that time is short, it will be many hours before I arrive into Chicago. There'll be stopovers, I'll have to change buses – there's a reason most people choose to fly in America over travelling long distances by road.

It will be arduous.

With such a long way to travel, and my photo all over the news, is there a chance I get recognised somewhere on the way? I fear there is and, without a decent disguise, I'm not putting up much resistance.

I need something. Anything.

Like a baseball cap.

I spot a guy standing outside the bus station, on the other side of the glass, smoking a cigarette. He's a burly man in his fifties, but he has my attention because of what he has on his head.

Figuring I have enough time, I pick up my bag and walk outside to see him, praying he hasn't seen the news today, or at least didn't pay enough attention to it to know that I'm the headline.

'Hi, sir. I was wondering, would you be willing to sell me your cap?'

The man turns to face me, letting out a puff of nicotine right in my face. I don't bat the smoke away. I just keep smiling to hopefully convince him that I'm a friendly, fun girl who just wants to make an innocent purchase.

'You want my cap?' the man replies in a slow, Southern drawl.

'Yes, please. I'm a big baseball fan and that's my favourite team,' I say, pointing to the colourful logo on the cap, even though I have no idea what I'm talking about. I just need something to convince him.

'It's not for sale,' the man replies, frowning and putting his cigarette back between his lips.

'Really? You won't take fifty dollars for it?' I ask, pulling out some cash from my pocket and flashing him a fifty.

I don't know this man's financial situation, but surely fifty dollars for an old, tatty cap is a good price, unless the cap has sentimental value, which I pray it does not. I really hope his father or grandfather didn't buy him this cap at his first ever ball game fifty years ago, or I'm screwed. But I guess not when the man looks at the money and smiles.

'For this old thing? Sure, why not?' he says before taking the cap off his head.

'Thank you!' I cry as I hand him his money. I take the cap and quickly apply it to my scalp, and I'm about to go back into the station when the man calls after me.

'It's a basketball team by the way,' he says, and as I look back at him, aware he caught me in a lie, he simply winks at me before going on his way.

Does he know why I needed this extra method of disguise? Or is he just playing with me?

I don't know and I'm definitely not going to hang around to find out.

I rush back into the station and plan on retaking my seat for the final few minutes before my bus is ready to accept passengers. Before I sit down, I glance up at the departure screen to see exactly how long I have left to wait. Four minutes, apparently, which would be fine.

But then I see what is on the screen beside it. It's footage from a house I recognise.

But it's not a house in Chicago.

It's a house right here in Florida.

I'm staring at a local news report now, and the top story is something else that involves me.

The house on screen is the house I was trapped in earlier today.

It's Parker's place.

'Now boarding for Chicago,' comes the call from a driver at the back of the station, and several already-weary travellers rise up from their seats, collect their luggage and start making their way to where they need to board. I guess I should join them. That's my bus too. But I don't.

I'm not moving a muscle.

That's because I'm still staring at the news report.

The one that says the homeowner involved in an incident to which police were called this morning, a Mr Parker White, is currently recovering in South Florida Hospital.

EPILOGUE

This place is familiar.

The long corridors. The uniforms. The fluorescent lighting. The sickly looking patients being wheeled past on squeaky trolley beds. The sense that nobody would willingly choose to spend their time here, yet some do.

For some, this place is a calling. A vocation. A chance to help others.

Some of those people are nurses.

People like me.

I don't know what I was in my past life, the life that existed in that space that my memory can no longer recall.

But I do know what I am now.

I am a woman planning on posing as a nurse to get closer to a particular patient.

I walked into this hospital two minutes ago, probably looking like somebody who belonged here. If anyone was to pay me any attention, they would presume I was a visitor on my way to see a patient, a loved one who was recuperating here. But I'm not. Not that it matters, because nobody is paying me any attention. This place is far too busy for people to stop and stare at me.

Medical staff rush around in between patients being pushed in wheelchairs and visitors grabbing some snacks from a vending machine before they head back to one of the wards. There's a lot going on here, as there is in any hospital across the world, and the constant chaos is allowing me to move unnoticed throughout much of it.

I move deeper into the hospital, leaving behind busy waiting rooms and making my way down corridors that seem to stretch endlessly into the distance. South Florida Hospital is a big place, making my task very much akin to finding a needle in a haystack.

I'm looking for Parker.

He just better hope that I can't find him.

However, a couple of things should help me to narrow down my search. First of all, I have an idea which department to go to. Thanks to the news, I know that Parker is still alive, though I saw him for myself lying on the carpet this morning and I know he suffered a serious injury. Therefore, he must be in intensive care, so I follow the signs on the wall for that part of the hospital. The other thing that should help me, at least partly, is knowing there will be a police presence around wherever Parker is located. The investigation into what happened at his home will be underway, and if Joe and Irene told the truth, Parker will be being treated as a criminal during his recovery.

If he recovers, that is.

But if he's alive, what's stopping him trying to talk his way out of what he did? He could lie, and someone as good at lying as him might just stand a chance of getting someone to believe him. Someone that matters, like a detective or a judge or a jury member. He is guilty as sin, but if he survives and gets better he might escape punishment altogether, and what would stop him from doing what he did to some other poor woman in future?

And what is stopping him coming after Irene again?

Or me?

Even if he didn't get away with it and ultimately faced jail time, would he try to bargain with the police for a lesser sentence? He certainly has some bargaining power with his experience meeting me. He could play his trump card, the one where he tells them that he knows all about me, the woman the Chicago PD are desperate to find, the one who is wanted for a double homicide that might remain unsolved unless I'm found. He could tell them what I've been doing, what I look like now, my last location, all things that could help close the net and see me incarcerated just like him.

He could be the reason for my downfall in so many different ways.

But not if I can help it.

The thought there are police officers lurking somewhere in this hospital, standing near to Parker as he recovers, only adds to my stress levels, but I'm going to forge on anyway because I cannot leave Florida without finishing this. I thought it already was finished. Joe certainly thought so when he told me his son was dead. I guess the paramedics found evidence of a heartbeat when they arrived at the scene.

If I have my way, there won't be a heartbeat for much longer.

I'm getting close to the intensive care ward now, but I'm dressed in plain clothes and that won't get me much further, especially not past the police, so I need to get changed. That's why, when I see a hospital employee ahead of me pushing a huge trolley filled with clothes, I follow them.

He leads me past the wards and away from the doctors and nurses, to a quieter part of the hospital where no patients are. This is a peek behind the scenes where staff like cleaners and janitors work discreetly in the background to make sure this hospital can operate. People like the guy in front of me are part of a team who helps wash the huge volume of bed linen here.

But he also washes something else.

The uniforms.

I can see several blue nurses' uniforms in his trolley, in amongst surgical scrubs, no doubt all worn by medical professionals who have recently finished their shifts and gone home. These uniforms will be washed and ready for them on their next shift, but one of them is about to be used again much sooner than that.

'Excuse me?' I call out to the man with the trolley, and he stops before reaching the laundrette to see me coming down the corridor towards him.

'Are you okay?' he asks me. 'You shouldn't be in this part of the hospital.'

'Yeah, sorry. I think I've got lost.'

The man buys my lie, probably because I'm not the first member of the public to go astray in this maze of corridors.

'No worries,' he says as I reach him and his overflowing trolley full of uniforms. 'Where are you trying to get to?'

'Ward B,' I say, purposely picking somewhere I know is a long way from here, because I remember passing that ward on the way in.

'Oh wow, you really are lost. That's all the way back there,' the man says, gesturing back the way I just came.

As he turns, I make sure to move a little closer to his trolley, but he's already looking back at me rather than down the corridor, so I need to try something else if I'm going to get the chance to steal from him.

'Sorry. I'm terrible with directions,' I say, playing dumb. 'Can you be more specific? Exactly which way do I need to go at the end of the corridor? Left or right?'

I gesture down the corridor again in the hope that it will

make the man slightly in front of me turn and look that way too, and sure enough he does.

'You go all the way to the end,' he says, his back now to me as he presumes I'm paying attention to his advice. 'And then when you get there, you turn left. After that, you need to walk for about five minutes, all the way to the front of the hospital again and then, when you see the large double doors, turn right and you'll be on Ward B. That clear enough?'

'That's absolutely perfect, thank you,' I say with a smile, but I'm not smiling because of how clear the instructions were.

I'm smiling because, while he was distracted, I was able to take a nurse's uniform from his trolley and hide it behind my back.

'Have a great day,' I say, still smiling as I keep the uniform hidden from the man, who puts his hands back on his heavy trolley and starts pushing again.

Only when it's safe do I bring the uniform out from behind my back and take a closer look at it.

This is perfect.

With this on, I will look like a nurse.

With this on, hopefully, nobody will suspect a thing.

I look around for a toilet, a private place, somewhere I can duck into to get changed, and then I find one. An empty cubicle is the perfect place for my costume alteration. With the uniform on, I smooth out a few of the creases on it before taking a look at my reflection in the mirror above the sink.

It's not a perfect fit and hangs a little loose, but I didn't expect it to be my exact size.

What's really bizarre is that I feel this look actually suits me, as if I'm supposed to wear something like this.

I guess that will help convince others that I should be wearing it too.

I leave the safety of the private room then, my bundle of

clothes hidden under a bed, and start walking in the direction of the ward I need. Each step I take makes the dread in my body grow stronger, and I'm still limping a bit from my injuries in that basement, though the adrenaline is helping me deal with that.

I walk on down another corridor, feeling like a fraud in this uniform, a fraud among these other medical experts, but I keep going until I see the sign for the ward where the patient is. If Parker knew I was here, he would panic, cry out for help, alert somebody to the fact that something is wrong. But they don't know I'm here. Not yet.

By the time they do, it will be too late.

As I turn a corner, I'm suddenly confronted with a nurse. She looks me right in the eyes, causing every cell in my body to tell me that this is it. This is where it's over. This is where I get punished for being here and pretending to be a proper nurse.

But nothing happens. The other nurse, the one who actually belongs here, just smiles at me before walking past, as if she didn't just see a ghost. Okay, so I'm not dead, so I'm not really a ghost, but I feel like one, haunting this hospital, destined for doom, because the longer I'm here, the less time I have to back out of this. Except I'm not backing out, and I know I'm close to where I need to be now – I see a police officer chatting to a doctor in the distance.

That police officer is here to see the same patient.

But I need to make sure I see them first.

I walk past the police officer and the doctor, either one of whom could suddenly ask me a question and cause me to have a panic attack. A simple question like, 'Where are you going?' would be enough to do it. Then, when they saw me crumble, they'd know I was a fraud, and the doctor would sound the alarm while the officer would reach for one of two things.

His handcuffs.

Or his gun.

But neither of them asks me anything, and why would they?

I'm just a nurse going about her work, on my way to see a patient, as busy as everybody else here, just grinding it out until the end of my shift.

And I am almost at the end now.

I enter the ward, doing my best to walk around the edges of it, by the walls, so I'm more discreet than if I was walking boldly down the centre of it. Now I'm here, I see half a dozen curtains around what I presume will be beds. There are patients behind all these curtains, six of them in total, all resting in privacy before they are poked and prodded during their next round of medical checks.

Is Parker here somewhere? Which curtain could he be behind?

Before I can find that out, I need to remain unseen from the two nurses I hear chatting in a room nearby. The door is open but they can't see me from where I'm hiding, though I can hear what they're saying. They're talking about a shift change, how one of them can't wait to go home because it's been a long day, and how another nurse is running late so the ward is temporarily short-staffed.

This sounds like a good time to make my move, while the ward is undermanned, and as I creep to the open door, I prepare to peep around the edges of it, in the hopes that the nurses inside are not looking in my direction. I have to pass this door to get to the patients, so there's no way around it. Holding my breath, I take a look.

It's a relief when I see two nurses at a desk with their backs to me, one of them typing on a computer while the other is writing something in a notebook. Neither of them know I'm standing right behind them, and now neither of them know I have just walked right past and no longer have any obstacles between myself and the patient I'm here to see.

My biggest problem now is figuring out which curtain Parker is behind.

Then I see a clipboard hanging on the wall.

I pick it up, take a look and I see that it helpfully lists all the various patients currently on this ward. It also lists their exact location. Bed 1, Bed 2 and so on. So is he here?

I scan the list for Parker's name and there it is.

He's here.

And he's in Bed 6.

I look across the ward and count the row of beds before realising that Parker's is the one right at the end in the back corner. Like all the other beds, the curtain is closed around it, which is perfect, so I put the clipboard back and double-check one more time that no nurses have spotted me before I start walking again.

As I go, passing the other curtains, I hear a few snores from sleeping patients. But my only concern is my patient, the one I am in charge of now, though the one who doesn't currently realise it.

I reach the curtain that separates me from Bed 6 and gently take hold of it. Then I take a deep breath before peeling it back slightly so I can get a look inside.

I'm checking to make sure there is nobody in here with Parker. The last thing I need is another nurse sitting by his bed – or worse, a police officer.

I need him to be alone.

And he is.

Parker is lying in the bed, his arms resting by his sides and his eyes closed. He is hooked up to an IV drip and there is a beeping machine beside him showing his heart rate and blood pressure. His stats look good, at least I think they do, but that's all about to change. Currently, he poses no threat, not to me or to any other women, but I know it would be very different if he wasn't in recovery. At full strength, this man is extremely dangerous, and in more ways than one. He tricked me, captured me, almost killed me and, if left to recuperate, he could help the police catch me and my family. It's frightening to be in his presence again so soon after he locked me in his basement, and I'd rather not be so close to him, but if I don't do this, I'll never be free from the fear of him.

I step past the curtain before closing it behind myself and, while the heartrate on the machine remains steady, my own is speeding up rapidly. It only beats stronger the closer I get to the bed, and when I pick up the spare pillow from the chair beside me, I feel like I'm on the verge of having a heart attack.

This is my last chance to turn around and get out of here.

If I take one more step, it'll be too late and there'll be no going back.

So I take it.

Before using the pillow, I carefully unplug the machines that Parker is hooked up to. Turning them off completely will limit the alerts sent to the nurses in that room when his vitals start crashing in a few moments' time. They might still be alerted, but it might not be quite as quick as if the machine was 'live' and the patient was crashing while still hooked up to it. I'm hoping this will buy me a little extra time to do what I need to do.

Once that's done and he's disconnected from the electronic equipment, I raise the pillow.

Breathing hard, I go to bring it down over Parker's face, reminding myself as I do about how he mocked me while I was trapped in his basement, how he pushed me down the stairs without regard for my health and how he tormented poor Irene for such a long time. This man deserves to die and, once this pillow is over his face, that is exactly what will happen.

The pillow is now inches away from going over his mouth and nose and stopping him breathing.

But just before that happens, something else does.

Parker opens his eyes.

He sees me and he recognises me. I'm pretty sure that if I

give him one more second, he'll call out for me to stop what I'm doing. I can't allow that – somebody else on this ward will hear him and I'll get caught before I finish what I've started.

So I force the pillow down over his face.

Then I grit my teeth and hold on to it tightly.

Parker's whole body is writhing on the bed as he fights for his life, his fingernails scratching at my arms while his legs are kicking uselessly, but his muffled screams are only audible to me, allowing me to keep working without too much noise. My victim is also weaker from his recent injuries, so he's struggling less than he otherwise might if fully fit, and I'm able to over-power him more and more easily as his already weak body futilely tries to fend me off.

I have tears in my eyes, not just because I'm taking a life, or because it's a stressful situation, but because there is a part of me that tells me I can do it.

I feel like I have experience of this.

I have killed before.

As Parker starts to lose his battle, the flashback I get is one I've never had before. I don't see Laurence or his ill wife or any needles. This time, I'm with someone else.

I'm suffocating somebody else.

Who is it?

I don't know because the pillow is over their face.

All I know is that I am young in the flashback, in my early twenties, possibly in nursing school.

And I'm killing somebody.

Did that really happen? Or was it my brain's way of trying to get me to cope with this crazy situation right here? I don't know for sure, but by the time I snap out of the flashback, I realise that Parker has stopped moving. That's my cue to get out of here as quickly as possible before any doctors and nurses come to check on this end of the ward.

Dropping the pillow and getting the briefest of glimpses of

Parker's lifeless face, I poke my head between the curtains to check if the coast is clear. It is, but I can hear some commotion at the far end. The new nurse has just arrived for her shift and I presume that means she'll be doing her rounds of the ward soon. When she does, she'll realise that they are now one patient light.

I need a way out, one that doesn't involve passing all those nurses and the police officer beyond them. Then I see a door to my left and I try it. It's unlocked, so I slip through it, but I don't have time to hang around, so I pick a direction to go in and start walking down another corridor.

As I go, I wonder how I'm ever going to be able to find the private room where I left my clothes to get changed again, but then I make the split-second decision to forget about getting changed.

I just need to get out of this hospital as fast as I can.

I walk quickly, ignoring my limp and the increasing amount of pain in my body from my fall down the stairs – I cannot risk being caught here.

Trespassing. Impersonating a nurse. Homicide.

The list of crimes I would be accused of if arrested is long and grave.

I keep moving, passing other nurses, one of whom gives me a confused glance as if she is wondering if she has seen me around here before or if I'm new. Or maybe she's thinking she recognises me from the latest news bulletins but isn't quite sure, because she only saw it briefly and she has a lot of other things on her mind. But I can't stop to let her ask me, nor can I stop when I see a group of doctors approaching. I definitely can't stop when I see a police officer pick up his radio and listen in.

Is he getting the alert that there is a killer nurse on the loose?

I don't care to know because I can see the exit now – those

sliding doors beyond which could be my freedom, if only I can make it in time.

I quicken my pace as my bruised ribs throb and my heart threatens to burst out of my chest. But on the surface, I just look like a nurse leaving a hospital.

So I guess that's why no one stops me.

The fresh air feels wonderful on my face and I'm still walking as quickly as I can. The further I go, the more I feel like I am going to get away with this.

By the time I board the almost-empty bus to take me away from the hospital, I am certain I have, at least for now. It's just me, the weary driver and a couple of distracted passengers staring at their phones and soon, once I disembark and vanish, it will just be me again.

But this is not over. Not really. I know the authorities still want me, not only here, but in Chicago.

They can keep looking for me.

While they do, I am going to look for my family.

I just hope I find them before the police do.

A LETTER FROM DANIEL

Dear reader,

I want to say a huge thank you for choosing to read *The Nurse's Lie*. I hope you enjoyed following Darcy and Pippa's journey! If you did enjoy it and would like to keep up to date with all my latest Bookouture releases, including future books in this particular series, please sign up at the following link. When you sign up you will receive a free short story, *The Killer Wife*. Your email address will never be shared and you can unsubscribe at any time.

www.bookouture.com/daniel-hurst

I hope you loved this second book in *The Perfect Nurse* series and, if you did, I would be very grateful if you could write an honest review. I'd like to hear what you think!

You can also visit my website where you can download a free psychological thriller called *Just One Second* and join my personal weekly newsletter, where you can hear all about my future writing as well as my adventures with my wife, Harriet, and daughter, Penny!

Thank you,

Daniel

KEEP IN TOUCH WITH DANIEL

Get in touch with me directly at my email address
daniel@danielhurstbooks.com. I reply to every message!

www.danielhurstbooks.com

 facebook.com/danielhurstbooks
instagram.com/danielhurstbooks

PUBLISHING TEAM

Turning a manuscript into a book requires the efforts of many people. The publishing team at Bookouture would like to acknowledge everyone who contributed to this publication.

Audio
Alba Proko
Melissa Tran
Sinead O'Connor

Commercial
Lauren Morrissette
Hannah Richmond
Imogen Allport

Cover design
Lisa Horton

Data and analysis
Mark Alder
Mohamed Bussuri

Editorial
Natasha Harding
Lizzie Brien

Printed in Great Britain
by Amazon

45825311R00148